PRELUDE TO MURDER

"I told you I'd give you money," Etta said. "Perhaps fifteen hundred?"

Dan shook his head. "I'm thinking in terms of twenty five to thirty thousand. For my son's life, which ended because of you. Long overdue and cheap at the price!"

"I couldn't give you that much! It's my security, my cushion!"

"You've had too much cushion in your life. It's time things were evened up. Of course, you do have a choice. You can hang on to your money and let me tell people how Jimmy died. You could never live it down in this respectable town. You'd have to pull up stakes and start all over again somewhere else. And I'd bide my time until you were settled, and then tell my story again. I'm making you a fair and square offer to buy my silence. If you don't accept it I'll keep on your trail—*till one of us is in our grave!*"

DORIS MILES DISNEY
THE MAGIC GRANDFATHER

ZEBRA BOOKS
KENSINGTON PUBLISHING CORP.

ZEBRA BOOKS

are published by

Kensington Publishing Corp.
475 Park Avenue South
New York, NY 10016

First Zebra Books printing: February, 1989

Printed in the United States of America

For Sarah Nuding,
age five,
whose headstands and opinions I hold in respect

CONTENTS

1952

Chapter 1

Her name was Sarah Prince. She was going on five, a sturdy, handsome child, a butterball of a child, silky to the touch with rosy silky skin and fine silky light hair forever slipping out of the two barrettes that were meant to hold it back off her round face. Her eyes were very big, very bright, very blue. She wore glasses to correct a small defect in them. The glasses had a habit of slipping down her button nose which did not have enough bridge to hold them up. She had a habit of looking at people over the tops of them with what her father called her Benjamin Franklin look of wisdom. She was wise — that is to say, intelligent — beyond her years. She had a vocabulary range beyond her years. She was utter charmer and stubborn mule by turns, an angel, a vixen. In short, a human being of few years but of definite engaging personality, the essence of what she would be all her days.

She had a father and mother who tempered adoration with realism; she had a brother Bobby who was eight and a sister Amy going on ten, both regarding her with much realism and very little adoration.

She lived in Harrington, in northwestern Connecticut, a thriving, self-contained community outside the orbit of turnpikes and parkways pointing to New York or Boston. It had a population of 11,500 or 12,000, depending on what statistics were used. (Never used by the townspeople themselves were the 1950 census figures. Harrington, they said, had grown by hundreds — or wasn't it close to a thousand? — since those figures were compiled.)

She lived on Bromfield Street in an outlying section of the town, a mixture of older houses, some of them once farms, and newer houses built just before or after World War II. Regardless of when they were built, they all stood on ample lots, none jostling another, and a few had fields around them. The Princes' seven-room ranch house, built in 1947, the year Sarah was born, had open land bordering it on the town side with their nearest neighbor, Mrs. Lane, a good three hundred feet away.

Sarah, on a pleasant March afternoon, went to visit Mrs. Lane, a gentle, undemanding woman, quiet and reserved herself, but a good listener. She was Sarah's favorite among the neighbors, letting her have the run of the house, giving her treats, fruit, cookies, an occasional candy bar to take home for after dinner.

Although she would have her fiftieth birthday in July, Henrietta Lane did not look anywhere near her age. She was still blonde and slim and lovely with a soft voice, an air of elegance, a flair for clothes, mostly tailored, and a closet full of them that Sarah was sometimes permitted to try on. Equally fascinating was the assortment of toiletries on her dressing table, creams, lotions, eye make-up, lipsticks of various shades to complement whatever color Mrs. Lane was wearing—Sarah's mother was the casual possessor of just one lipstick at a time—perfumes and colognes. There was nothing the little girl enjoyed more than watching Mrs. Lane get dressed for some special occasion and painstakingly and discreetly apply just the right amount of make-up to enhance her youthful appearance.

For reasons of this sort and for the basic reason that they enjoyed each other's company, it had become Sarah's custom in the past few months since she had been permitted to leave her own yard to visit Mrs. Lane two or three times a week. Sometimes, after staying only a few minutes, she would announce that she was going home; other times Mrs. Lane would tell her she was too busy for company or was going out herself. Either way, there were no hard feelings; they had an excellent understanding of each other.

On that particular March afternoon Mrs. Lane said that Mrs. Bartlett, their neighbor from up the street, was coming over for coffee at four o'clock but that Sarah could stay until she arrived.

The little girl didn't like Mrs. Bartlett who tended to ignore her.

"What's she coming for?" she asked.

"Well . . ." Mrs. Lane, about to explain the Garden Club's spring tour and the committee work involved, hesitated, thinking of the cross-examination that might come from Sarah. Then, reaching for the percolator, she said firmly, "We're going to be working together for a club we belong to."

"Oh." Sarah's tone indicated total lack of interest. She had come in the back door and her eye had just fallen on a frosted cake on the counter. "You going to give her a piece of that cake?"

"Yes." Mrs. Lane threw a smile over her shoulder. "And if you're a very good girl I'll give you a piece before you go home."

"I'm always a good girl," Sarah stated without regard for the truth.

"Most of the time," Mrs. Lane amended. She looked around for her cigarettes as she measured coffee into the percolator basket. "Honey, will you please go see if I left my cigarettes in the living room?"

"Uh-huh." Sarah trotted up the hall pausing in the living-room doorway to push up her glasses. The cigarettes lay on a table near the front window. She looked out the window as she picked them up and saw an elderly man, carrying a large suitcase, walking toward the house. There were no sidewalks this far out from the center. He walked at the edge of the road, stopping to shift the suitcase from one hand to the other and stopping again in front of Mrs. Lane's to look at the house number. He set down his suitcase and turned to face the house, glance appraising it, a comfortable, roomy clapboard house built in the early 1900s when front porches were still in vogue, a well-kept house, surrounded by a lawn and shrubbery, a sun porch on one side and an amesite driveway on the other leading to a two-car garage in the rear.

When the man had looked his fill he took off his hat, revealing a thick crop of white hair, and wiped

14

his forehead as if perspiring from the weight of the suitcase or some other cause. He put away his handkerchief, picked up the suitcase and started up the front walk.

Sarah darted out to the kitchen crying, "Mrs. Lane, you got comp'ny. There's a—a—grandfather man coming up the walk. He's got a suitcase. Maybe he's coming to stay."

Mrs. Lane laughed. "Probably selling something," she said plugging in the percolator. "Suitcase full of samples, I don't doubt."

Footsteps sounded on the porch. The doorbell rang. Mrs. Lane, with Sarah tagging after her, went to answer it.

She did not recognize the tall old man at first but he knew her instantly, the slim blonde woman who wore her simple wool dress with style, whose hair seemed unfaded and face not too much older looking than the last time he had seen it nearly twenty-seven years ago. There wasn't the least doubt that this was Etta who had once been his daughter-in-law.

He took off his hat, swept it off, rather, as if on stage, revealing again his handsome white head. "Well, Etta," he said. "How are you?"

She could not believe it was the man she thought it was. She put on her glasses, suspended on a chain around her neck, and stared at him, her face losing color as she studied his lined face, brown eyes sharp as ever peering out from under heavy white brows, a smile, half uncertain, half triumphant touching the corners of his thin-lipped mouth.

She stared without hope that it was someone else. It was Jimmy's father. It was Dan Ferris. She had not seen him since the night she fled Grayport, Illinois, on the midnight bus hoping never to lay eyes on him again.

Now, like a ghost risen from the dead, he stood on her doorstep, a figure from the past she never let herself think of, the tragic, shameful past buried twenty-seven years ago, buried, she had hoped, forever.

She would have let the storm door slam in his face if he had not caught hold of it.

His smile broadened. "Aren't you going to invite me in, Etta? Not very polite to keep me standing on the doorstep." He stepped over the threshold as he spoke coming so close that she had to draw back to avoid contact with him.

He let his glance stray to Sarah who eyed him doubtfully, aware of the complete lack of welcome in Mrs. Lane's attitude.

"And who might this young lady be?" he inquired. "Don't tell me you've made me a—well, grandfather-in-law, shall we say?"

Mrs. Lane recovered the use of her voice. "Hardly," she replied. "Or have you forgotten my age?"

"No, I haven't forgotten it." He looked her up and down, his eyes suddenly cold. "I haven't forgotten anything about you, Etta. All these years by myself you've stayed green in my memory. Who did you say this was?"

"Sarah Prince, a neighbor's child." As the little girl looked up at her questioningly Mrs. Lane tried to turn it into an ordinary introduction. "Sarah, this is Mr. Ferris," she said.

"Mrs. Lane's father-in-law, that's what I am or used

to be, Sarah," the old man amplified. He gave her a pleasant, even winning, smile but she did not return it. She went on looking at him doubtfully, glasses far down on her nose.

He skirted around the woman and child and stood in the middle of the hall, taking in the living room that opened off it on his right, the carpeted stairway going up the outside wall, the kitchen at the far end.

"Nice place you've got here, Etta," he said over his shoulder. "Comfortable. But have you ever thought of having all this oak woodwork painted white? Dates the house, you know."

She did not answer. Taut and pale she looked at him. Sarah pressed against her, eying her in puzzlement over the stiffness of her whole body.

The old man set his suitcase down near the staircase, strolled through the archway into the living room and gave it a leisurely inspection, glancing through the inner door at the dining room and the sun porch beyond.

"Nice place," he said again. "The fireplace adds to it. Nothing like an open fire on a cold winter night. Use it a lot?"

"We did when my husband was alive," she said through dry lips. "Not so much by myself."

"Oh yes," he said. "You're a widow again, I understand."

"Yes, I am." She swallowed to moisten her mouth. "Since a year ago January," she said.

But what made her say it, pick up her end of the conversation as if they were just old acquaintances meeting by chance?

What did he want from her? Money—revenge, in-

17

tent to wreck her life by spreading around the story of the past? Or was it both?

Her heart hammered. She became aware of Sarah, stirring uneasily beside her. She thought of the prim, correct Mrs. Bartlett due to arrive any moment now.

First she must get rid of Sarah; then she could try to get Dan Ferris out of the house before Mrs. Bartlett's arrival.

She could try but just looking at him told her she would not succeed. He took off his overcoat, laid it aside with his hat and sat down in an armchair with the air of one prepared to stay.

"Sarah." She touched the little girl's shoulder. "Perhaps you'd better run along home now."

"Uh-huh." Sarah's eyes were glued to the old man. She had dropped her jacket on the sofa when she was in the living room earlier and went to get it, halting midway in the room to look back at Mrs. Lane. "You said I could have a piece of cake first," she reminded her.

"Oh yes. I'll cut it for you now and you can eat it on the way home."

Mrs. Lane retreated to the kitchen, welcoming the respite it gave her, the chance to collect herself, gird herself, rather, before she had to face the old man again.

The coffee was perking briskly. It seemed unbelievable that she had plugged it in only a few minutes ago with nothing of consequence on her mind.

Her hands trembled as she got out a knife to cut the cake. She stood with it in her hand looking at it unseeingly.

What did he want? How had he found her?

In the living room Sarah perched on the edge of the sofa staring at the old man.

"So your name is Sarah Prince," he said. "How can it be Prince when you're a girl? Shouldn't it be princess?"

She giggled and shook her head. "It's not prince like in a fairy tale. It's just my last name."

"I know, but it doesn't seem right, a girl called prince."

This time Sarah found the comment hilarious, laughing so hard that tears ran down her cheeks. Brushing them away she said, "You're a funny man."

"Am I?" He gave her a roguish grin. "That used to be my business, princess — entertaining people. Princess — that'll be my name for you — Sarah Princess. D'you like it, Miss Princess?"

Fresh gales of laughter swept away the doubt Mrs. Lane's attitude toward him had aroused in her. She waited expectantly for him to make her laugh again.

Instead, he eyed her gravely and asked, "Did you ever see anyone wiggle their ears?"

She shook her head.

"Come here, then, princess, and I'll show you how it's done."

She got up from the sofa and went over to him. He held out his hand. "Press my knuckle, the first one."

She pressed it and watched spellbound his ears wiggle up and down. When they stopped she pressed his knuckle again and his ears wiggled again.

"Show me how to do it." She held out her hand. He pressed the dimpled flesh but for all her effort her ears did not move.

"You can't do it, you see," he said solemnly. "I'm

the only one."

She edged closer and while he pretended to look away pressed the knuckle of his second finger. Nothing happened.

"Has to be the first one, princess," he said.

She pressed the first knuckle. His ears wiggled.

Mrs. Lane reappeared carrying a slice of cake wrapped in wax paper. "Here you are, Sarah." She laid it down, helped her into her jacket and handed the cake to her.

"Thank you," said Sarah heading toward the kitchen because she always came and went by the back door. She got as far as the hall, turned back to the old man and pressed his knuckle. His ears moved up and down. With a last fascinated look at them she said good-by and rushed out the back door forgetting, in her excitement, to close it but not failing to hear the old man call after her, "Be seeing you, princess."

She could hardly wait to get home. She ran all the way with only one stop for a bite of cake. A piece broke off and fell on the road and in her haste she almost didn't take time to scoop it up and cram it into her mouth.

She burst into the house shouting before she looked to see if there was anyone in the kitchen, "Mommy, Mommy, there's a magic grandfather over at Mrs. Lane's house!"

Her mother listened as she poured out her story and looked impressed. Her sister Amy and brother Bobby looked bored in keeping with their age advantage over Sarah.

"Huh," said Bobby, "it's just a silly old trick."

"I bet loads of people can wiggle their ears," said Amy. "Loads and loads. Millions, maybe," she added as an afterthought.

But Sarah was not so easily squelched. She had learned long ago, as the youngest in any family must, not to allow herself to be. She went on to her bedroom, shared with Amy, and stood in front of the mirror, pressing her knuckle, trying to wiggle her ears. She wrinkled her forehead into ridges, her eyebrows rose in arcs above her glasses, she puffed from the strain until her face turned red but her ears stayed immovable against her head.

Maybe, though, if she just kept trying . . .

That night she called her father into the bathroom while she was in the tub, held out her hand and said, "Press my knuckle."

He pressed. She blinked her eyes as fast as she could.

"See," she said, "I'm magic too."

Just before she fell asleep that night she remembered that the old man hadn't said good-by when she left. Be seeing you, he had said.

P'raps he was going to stay at Mrs. Lane's, she thought hopefully. He'd brought his suitcase. P'raps he was going to stay forever.

It was a lovely thought, the magic grandfather staying forever. She hugged it to her as she went to sleep.

Chapter 2

They looked at each other in silence after Sarah left. Then Mrs. Lane said, "I didn't hear her shut the back door," and went out to the kitchen.

The old man was just emerging from the sun porch when she returned to the living room.

"Real nice, the whole place," he said. "Yessiree. You did all right for yourself, Etta. You certainly did."

"Did I?" She stood in the doorway and said with more firmness than she felt, "What brought you here? What do you want?"

"Now Etta." He gave her a reproving glance. "That's no way to greet your father-in-law, is it? After all these years too." He tipped his head to one side contemplatively—she had forgotten that bird-like habit of his that had irritated her in the old days—and produced a coaxing grin. "A small welcome mat at the door—I'm at least entitled to that, wouldn't you say?"

"You're entitled to nothing from me," she replied trying to keep the firmness she did not feel in her voice. "Nothing at all."

"Haven't changed a bit, have you?" He still wore

the grin but his eyes turned cold above it. "You never liked me and you never tried very hard to hide it."

"You know why." She could bring out into the open part of the reason, the part he already knew. "Because you wouldn't let Jimmy go; because you wouldn't listen when he talked about breaking away from vaudeville, settling down and making a home for us. You knew vaudeville was on its way out but you wouldn't admit it, wouldn't give us a chance to have a normal life. You—" she broke off hearing her voice shake with the old frustrated anger from long ago. What was she thinking to let herself get led into a senseless argument about an issue as dead as Jimmy himself?

"You'll have to leave now," she said. "I'm having company."

"Oh, so that's who the coffee's for." He sniffed appreciatively. "Smells good. You won't begrudge me a cup, I hope." He settled himself in the chair he had vacated. "I've had a long bus ride, Etta, all the way from Altoona, Pennsylvania. Changing buses, sitting in waiting rooms—I'm not as young as I was. Takes it out of me nowadays."

"There are a couple of nice restaurants here in town where you can get something to eat and all the coffee you want. If you're short of money—" she broke off again. She was making another mistake.

"Oh, not so short that I couldn't buy myself a meal," he said airily. "By no means."

She looked at him in despair. Leah Bartlett was due to arrive and she had never mentioned his existence to her or anyone in Harrington.

As if reading her mind he said, "Don't worry about me putting my foot in it in front of your friends. I'll go along with whatever story you've told about your first husband. I'm a reasonable man," he paused, "as long as other people are reasonable with me."

There was no missing the threat behind the mildness. But what answer could she make to it?

A car stopped outside. She looked out the window. It was Leah Bartlett.

He eyed her in amusement. "Your friends arriving?"

"It's just one, a woman who's serving on a committee with me." She added hurriedly, "People here think Jimmy died in a car accident. I've never mentioned you at all."

"I see." He was plainly enjoying the sense of power he had over her. "Well, as I said, I'm a reasonable man. I won't spill the beans."

The doorbell rang. Mrs. Lane answered it and greeted her neighbor as pleasantly as if she hadn't a care in the world.

Dan Ferris got to his feet when they entered the room. Mrs. Bartlett, although she lived only a few blocks away, was as hatted and gloved and groomed as if attending a formal tea. She was that kind of a woman. No one ever heard her raise her reedy voice or saw her lose her unruffled manner. She sealed herself off from the coarser emotions. They weren't ladylike.

Scrawny-thin, bloodless looking, she made Mrs. Lane, with her rounded slimness and still youthful appearance, seem even more attractive than she was.

"Leah, this is Mr. Ferris, my first husband's father," she said.

"How do you do, Mr. Ferris," said Mrs. Bartlett, not permitting herself to show surprise at this unheralded arrival of a figure from out of Mrs. Lane's past. "Nice weather we're having for this time of year, isn't it?"

"Yes indeed." He bowed with practiced ease. His voice had not lost the resonance with which he had projected it to the back of the house in countless small-time theaters across the land.

Etta Lane tried to see him through Mrs. Bartlett's eyes. Neatly, if inexpensively, dressed in a dark suit, recent haircut, shoes well shined, generally presentable appearance—but then, no matter how lean his purse, he had always put on a good front. She had nothing to worry about in that direction, only about what he might say.

It was soon apparent, however, that he had no present intention of doing her injury. He turned on his charm, the easy charm that had never really taken her in, not even at nineteen when she first met him, her new father-in-law, nearly thirty years ago.

It softened Mrs. Bartlett's primness. She was a native of Harrington and it gratified her civic pride to be told she lived in one of the loveliest towns Dan Ferris had ever been in, a picture postcard town, he said, with its tree-shaded green, fine old houses and up-to-date business center. While Mrs. Lane poured coffee he confided to Mrs. Bartlett his great pleasure in seeing his daughter-in-law again.

"After my son Jimmy died—a great shock coming so suddenly in the flush of his youth—"

"Your only child, Mr. Ferris?" Mrs. Bartlett asked sympathetically.

"Yes, yes, the only one. I lost his mother in the flu epidemic of 1918 and never remarried. We had a marriage made in heaven, dear lady, and I never thought of putting anyone else in her place. I had Jimmy. I made him my whole life."

"How sad to lose him like that. These car accidents—" Mrs. Bartlett shook her head. "Was he killed instantly?"

"Yes, instantly." The old man shot a stern glance at Etta Lane. "A thing you never get over. The end of the world, so to speak, when it's your only child."

"I know," said Mrs. Bartlett who could not know, being childless.

"Etta and I lost track of each other soon afterwards and I was on my own."

"What a shame." Mrs. Bartlett looked at Etta Lane. She did not allow herself to show reproach but she looked at her.

"Just by chance," the old man continued, "I ran into a mutual friend of ours in Altoona—I've been living there the past few years—and he said he'd run into Etta somewhere a couple of years before and told me where she was living and what her name was now and well"—he divided a broad smile between the two women—"I said to myself, 'You're getting on, Dan Ferris, and before it's too late go pay a visit to your daughter-in-law, the only tie you have left.' So I packed my suitcase and got on a bus and here I am. Etta couldn't believe her eyes when she saw me on her doorstep."

"She must have been surprised," said Mrs. Bartlett. "Are you planning to stay a while, Mr. Ferris?"

The old man chuckled. "I guess you'd better ask Etta that. It's for the hostess to say, not the guest. I wouldn't want to stay until I wore out my welcome."

"Well . . . " Mrs. Lane smiled vaguely and left it at that evading his intent to box her into a corner, make her commit herself in front of Leah Bartlett who would, he knew, tell people of his arrival and that he was expected to stay.

He was as sly, as clever as he had always been at getting his own way but this time it wasn't going to work. She couldn't stand the sight of him; he made her flesh creep. She wouldn't have him in her house and would tell him so the moment Leah left.

She fortified herself with these thoughts as she poured him another cup of coffee but underneath was the chill doubt that it would be that easy to make him go.

Conversation flowed effortlessly between him and Mrs. Bartlett. He talked knowledgeably about gardening when she mentioned the spring garden tour. Perhaps he had worked for some nursery or landscape gardener along the way. He must have had many jobs, Mrs. Lane thought, since vaudeville, the only world he knew, failed him. He couldn't have made much money; there must have been times when he had to scratch for a living.

This thought brought a flicker of pity for him. She would write him a check for a hundred or two before she sent him on his way.

She was roused from her musings by the realization that he had moved onto dangerous ground. "Oh yes," he was saying to Mrs. Bartlett. "All my life from the time I was a kid of fourteen and saw this magician perform at the old Bijou back home. The bug bit me then and when it turned out that he needed an assistant I said I was sixteen and he took me on. I was a big kid for my age and he didn't question me much. I was with him four or five years but watching and learning and thinking about being on my own. Then I met my wife—we were playing Knoxville that week—and the first thing we knew we were married, just a couple of kids, and working out our own song and dance act. She was a better dancer than I was, trained from childhood for it, but I had plenty of brass and we got by and took Jimmy into the act with us—'The Three Ferrises' we called ourselves—as soon as he was old enough to tap out a few steps. Then, after my wife died, I worked up a specialty act—"

"Won't you have more coffee, Leah?" Mrs. Lane broke in hurriedly. "Did you like the cake? It's a new recipe I got from Mrs. Webster at library board meeting."

"Delicious," Mrs. Bartlett said.

"Another piece?"

"No, thank you. Much too near dinnertime."

"So simple to make too. You don't have to cream the sugar and butter first or separate the eggs. You just—"

The old man leaned back in his chair, his malicious smile telling her that he had come to the end of what he intended to say and that she had panicked unnecessarily.

She could not talk about the cake recipe forever. Presently Mrs. Bartlett found an opening to turn the conversation back to him.

"I've never known anyone who was on the stage before," she said. "Such a different kind of life, I imagine. But didn't you find it hard to turn to something else, Mr. Ferris, when movies put an end to vaudeville?"

"Well, I missed it, of course, the laughter, the applause, the excitement of holding an audience in the palm of my hand—"

The sticks, thought Etta Lane. Roll up into one the theaters they had played, the three-a-dayers, the small-time dingy theaters, smelling backstage of dirt and greasepaint, stale hope, stale sweat, unrealized dreams; roll up into one the cheap rooming houses and cafeterias, the day coaches ridden in the night with faces drained to death masks from exhaustion; roll up into one the lethargic audiences, the inert dwindling mass that, toward the end, came to see the feature picture and barely tolerated the vaudeville acts between; roll up into one the uncertainties, the living on the edge of financial nothingness, the besieging of agents for bookings, the magic that soon rubbed off, the enduring that set in, first for Jimmy's sake and then out of hopelessness.

Let him spin his lies and Leah Bartlett believe them. Let her go home and the showdown come with this man who had been her father-in-law.

". . . all my connections," he was saying. "No problem at all. A comedown, of course, from acting to being manager of a movie theater but at least it's kept me comfortable, dear lady, and I guess that's a lot at my age. And I have my press notices, scrapbooks full of them, to relive the triumphs of the past when the mood is on me."

So that was what he'd done all these years, Mrs. Lane thought relievedly. He'd always been careful with money—a precarious youth, he used to say, had taught him its value—and as manager of a movie theater, he was probably comfortably situated. She would not repeat her offer of money. She would just tell him to go.

If only Leah would leave; but in her prim way she seemed to find the old man's reminiscences fascinating.

As Sarah had; as people always had. He could charm the birds out of the trees with that smooth tongue of his Jimmy would say of his father in admiration touched with envy.

But he had never charmed her, not even at first when she and Jimmy were just married and she was eager to share his affection for the man he had described to her as his friend and partner as well as father.

She had soon learned to fear and dislike him. He became a sore point between Jimmy and her.

"But your son didn't stay in vaudeville, did he, Mr. Ferris?" Mrs. Bartlett inquired.

"Well, when he grew up—" The old man hesitated looking to Mrs. Lane for guidance.

She made haste to cover his pause. "I don't believe the subject ever came up with you, Leah," she said, "but Jimmy was a car salesman when we were married. We lived in Ohio and didn't see much of Dan who was on the road most of the time."

She had called him by name for the first time since his arrival. (Call me Dan, he had said, when Jimmy brought her, his bride, backstage to meet his father. None of that Mr. Ferris stuff, he had said. We're going to be friends, you and I. Nothing like a beautiful blonde for a daughter-in-law. He had taken her hand in both of his, kissed her on the cheek, smiled and winked, not seeming to resent his son's elopement with her.)

"But I used to get to that little apartment you and Jimmy had whenever I could," the old man said picking up his cue. "Always thought of it as home base."

(If you'll just break away from your father, get out of show business, she had pleaded with Jimmy. If you'll just get a steady job we could take a little apartment and settle down.)

If. Two-letter word, pot of gold at the end of the rainbow.

If Leah would just go home.

She left a few minutes later. "I know you and Mr. Ferris must have a lot to catch up on after all these years apart," she said. "We'll discuss the garden tour some other time, Etta."

The old man was instantly on his feet, light and quick as he had always been.

(How old was he now? Seventy-four? Seventy-five?)

Somehow he pre-empted the role of host. It was he who walked to the door with Mrs. Bartlett, took her gloved hand and said, "It's been a great pleasure, dear lady. You've been more than kind listening to an old man's reminiscences."

"I've enjoyed it," she replied. "I'll hope to see you again while you're visiting Etta. I know my husband would enjoy meeting you. He's made a hobby of amateur theatricals all his life and always gets a lead part when the Lions Club puts on a fund-raising show. Years ago, when they staged minstrels, he was end man. So you'd have a lot in common, you see."

"Yes indeed," said the old man with dead-pan face. "Minstrels. Amateur theatricals. Very interesting."

She was gone at last. He closed the door after her and turned back to Mrs. Lane who stood in the living room.

"What a stupid woman," he remarked. "Too stupid to know she was insulting me. Amateur shows. Me, that had top billing—"

"You never had top billing in your life," Mrs. Lane said in a flat voice.

He was taken aback for a moment. Then his face darkened. "You don't know what you're talking about. I was past my peak when the black day came that Jimmy married you."

She could have retorted that Jimmy had told her there'd never been a peak, nothing much better than what she had known with them herself. But she held it back. She didn't want to start an argument. She just wanted him to go.

He read the thought on her face. He sat down and said almost placatingly, "No hard feelings, Etta, when I've just arrived to pay you a visit."

"You can't," she said in the same flat voice. "It's out of the question. Go back to Altoona to your theater manager's job."

"Theater manager." He laughed derisively. "You're as gullible as your friend. I never was one." He leaned forward and gave her a level look. "I was done, washed up after what happened in Grayport. I took tickets in a crummy little movie house in a Chicago alley. That was the best I could do, Etta. Thanks to you. Nobody else. Just you. They let me go when I was seventy. Past three years I've been drifting around scraping up odd jobs to eke out my social security. Lately it's been Altoona, carrying out groceries, cutting people's lawns, anything I could get, trying"—he let a quaver come into his voice—"to keep body and soul together. That's what I've come to, Etta, thanks to you. The least you owe me, I figure, is the comfort of a visit and three home-cooked meals a day. I'm old, washed up. I need to take it easy for a while. So let's have no more talk about how I can't stay."

"You can't," she said. "You just can't."

She stood in the doorway very pale, eyes enormous, blue as ever, not faded, not changed, her dress picking up and accenting their color. She hadn't lost her looks or figure. In a different mature way she was still lovely, damn her to hell. How long was it she'd said her second husband was dead? How long before a prospective third came along?

"When did you say your second husband died?" he inquired.

"A year ago January."

"There'll be another. You're still a good-looking woman and always will be. You've got the bone structure for it. Your looks landed you in one soft nest and they'll land you in another. Different from

33

me. I was finished after what happened to Jimmy but you could make a fresh start, cover it all up, land on easy street. Just goes to show," he tried to speak lightly but there was venom in his tone, "that there's no justice in the world."

"I want you to go," she said. "I want nothing to do with you."

"You don't say?" He leaned back and crossed his legs. "If wishes were horses beggars could ride, Etta." He was suddenly enjoying himself, a twinkle in his eyes. "You must have a spare bedroom or two. Why don't you go upstairs and fix one up for me? While you're wasting time arguing about it, Mrs. Bartlett is probably on the phone telling people about your father-in-law arriving for a visit. Think of the talk if I vanished right away. They'd wonder about it. They'd say you must be covering up something to get rid of me so fast."

"I don't care what they say. I just want you to go. Look, I can spare a few hundreds to tide you over for now. And then why don't you apply to a retirement home for actors? I should think you would have done it long ago."

"Homes for the homeless, the broken-down actors," he said softly. "Doesn't it occur to you that it might revive the old scandal if I did it?"

"Of course not. They'd just take you in."

"Would they? And how would you like it if I gave your name as next of kin, Etta? Maybe they'd inquire about you here in Harrington. Lots of red tape, I'm sure. No thank you, I don't want that and neither do you once you stop to think it over. I'll just stay here a little while."

"No, no," she said desperately. "I'll give you a check now and I'll send you something every month to add to your social security. But you can't stay here. I won't have it."

"Get a room somewhere, that's what you mean." His voice was still soft. "A little bigger and better than the one I had in Altoona but that's all. Not a home, a room."

He stood up slowly. "If that's what you want Etta. But first, maybe, I'll stay at the inn downtown for tonight. And tomorrow, maybe, I'll call on your friend Mrs. Bartlett and reminisce some more about the old days. Maybe I'll show her some of the clippings from Grayport. Give the old bag something to talk about besides her husband's amateur theatricals."

She sagged in defeat as he reached for his hat and coat. He would do what he said. He was full of hate and malice, this old man, the poison of loss and failure. He tried to fasten all the blame on her but inside himself knew better and hated her the more for it.

He would ruin her if she sent him away. Years of living down the past, establishing a flawless reputation as Ed's wife would be swept away in minutes by a few words and some yellowed newspaper clippings.

It wasn't fair that all this and everything else she had done to improve herself, the organized reading program, the college courses taken at night, the time given to club and civic enterprises could be swept away in minutes. Ten or fifteen minutes was all that was needed to undo the efforts of half a lifetime. It wasn't fair but it was true. The old man had her trapped.

"All right," she said quietly, "you can stay for a few days. I'll make up a room for you."

She did not look at him as she turned and went upstairs. She did not want him to see how close she was to tears.

He stood in the doorway and looked after her in triumph.

Chapter 3

"Wanna see me do a headstand?"

"A headstand? Well, what do you know." The old man looked amazed. "I certainly would like to see it."

"I have to take my barrettes off first." Sarah took them off and handed them to him in a confiding gesture. "They hurt my head when I stand on it," she explained.

She had arrived a few minutes before, having told her mother she was going to Mrs. Lane's to see the magic grandfather. There had been some doubt in her mother's mind.

"If Mrs. Lane has company perhaps she'd rather not have you running in this morning," she said.

"She'll tell me," Sarah pointed out. "She always tells me if she doesn't want me to stay."

"Even so, I'll just call her." Her mother picked up the kitchen phone.

When Mrs. Lane answered she said, "Virginia Prince, Mrs. Lane. Sarah wants to pay you a visit but I understand you have company and I thought I'd better check first. Is it all right?"

"Perfectly all right. Tell her to come along."

Sarah's mother nodded to her. The little girl already had her jacket on and raced out the back door. Curiosity led her mother to add, "She came home yesterday all excited about your visitor. A magic grandfather, she said, whose ears wiggled when she pressed his knuckle." Virginia Prince laughed and drew a polite echo of laughter from Mrs. Lane who said, "She has quite an imagination."

There was the least silence. The older woman realized she would have to say more about the old man, be matter-of-fact, as if she had nothing to hide.

"Sarah's magic grandfather was my first husband's father," she said. "We've been out of touch for years. It was quite a surprise to have him turn up yesterday from out of the blue."

She could not infuse her tone with warmth. It registered on Virginia that it hadn't been a particularly pleasant surprise. Well, why should it be? she thought. Why should she welcome a visit from someone who could only bring back sad memories? Perhaps she didn't even like him; otherwise, she would have kept in touch with him.

"It must have been a surprise," she said, her own tone as neutral as Mrs. Lane's. Although they had been neighbors for five years she didn't feel that she knew the older woman well enough to offer further comment on her uninvited guest. It wasn't just the age difference between them; she could not have named anyone among Mrs. Lane's contemporaries who was her close friend; for all that she was pleasant to everyone, had a wide circle of acquaintances and was active in community affairs, there was a reserve in her manner that tended to keep people at a certain distance.

It was the first time Virginia Prince had ever given this a thought. Turning it over in her mind she said, "Send Sarah home, please, in half an hour. It's too nice out for her to stay indoors underfoot."

Mrs. Lane said she would and they hung up.

Sarah did her headstand in the living room with the old man her sole audience. It was one of her best efforts. Sometimes her legs wouldn't stay straight up in the air but this time they did. She held them up as long as she could, then rolled over in a somersault and came back up on her feet, hair in her eyes, face scarlet from the rush of blood to her head.

The old man applauded. "Wonderful," he said. "An acrobat couldn't do better."

"Maybe not as good," said Sarah unhampered by false modesty. "I wish Mrs. Lane saw it."

She ran out into the kitchen brushing back her hair. "I did a perfect headstand, Mrs. Lane, but you didn't even see it. Now I'm going to do a handstand. Come watch."

Mrs. Lane came as far as the doorway. She did not look at the old man. She kept her gaze on Sarah as she walked on her hands and when her glasses fell off said sharply, "Look out for your glasses, Sarah."

She was acting funny this morning, the little girl thought.

A moment later, aware of it herself, Mrs. Lane told her to get her barrettes, fastened back her hair and offered a cooky.

That was more like it. It turned out to be two cookies which Sarah ate in the kitchen. Then she returned to the living room. The old man was reading the paper. She edged up to him and pressed his knuckle. He seemed not to notice her but his ears wiggled. She shrieked with delight.

He laid the paper aside. "Know what I have upstairs,

39

princess?"

"What?"

"A magic coat. Want me to go put it on?"

She had no idea what a magic coat was but her eyes went big at the prospect. "Oh yes," she said.

While he was upstairs she ran out to Mrs. Lane. "A magic coat," she announced breathlessly. "He's going to put it on." She caught her hand. "Come and see."

Mrs. Lane started to demur, but then looked down at Sarah's glowing face reflecting that she mustn't turn the child against her over Dan Ferris.

"All right," she said and took her hand and went to the living room with her.

The old man came bouncing down the stairs in a dilapidated black coat rusty with age.

"Blanchard's," he informed Mrs. Lane. "Remember him? On the same bill with us in Rushville. This was his old one, his spare. I borrowed it to wear to that birthday party for Flo and then later, after what happened to Jimmy, I never got around to giving it back to him."

"I can't imagine why you kept it all these years." She eyed it with fastidious distaste.

"Ah, but you've had more luck than I've had, Etta." He gave her his sly needling grin. "You can turn your nose up at it but I couldn't afford to. It's brought in a few dollars now and then entertaining at children's parties."

Mrs. Lane made no answer. Sarah, waiting expectantly, looked at them over the rims of her glasses, not really listening to what they said but feeling vaguely uncomfortable over their attitude toward each other.

The old man dispelled this feeling as he turned his attention to her. "Well now," he said, "let's see what

40

kind of magic we'll do. It's all in the coat, princess. It gives me magic powers. Etta, could I borrow an egg?"

"I'll get it." Sarah rushed out to the kitchen and came back with an egg.

"Thank you," said the old man. "Put it in my pocket" — he pulled it open — "but first make sure it's empty."

She thrust her hand in. "There's a handkerchief," she said and took it out.

"Oh yes." It vanished up his sleeve. She put the egg in its place.

He reached into his pocket to take it out. A surprised look came over his face.

"It's not there," he said. "What'd you do with it, princess? Come on, give it to me."

"I haven't got it. See?" She held out her hands. "I put it in your pocket."

"It's not there now."

She couldn't believe it. She plunged her hand into his empty pocket and looked up at him open-mouthed, her face mirroring her astonishment and confusion.

"You took it out, Mr. Ferris," she said. "You're teasing me. It's in your other hand."

"No, it's not." He held out both hands.

She shot a questioning glance at Mrs. Lane who smiled and said, "I don't have it, Sarah."

"It must be around somewhere." The old man pointed to a pot of ivy on the window sill. "Did you look in the ivy?"

Sarah looked. The egg was there nestled among the leaves.

She was speechless, saucer-eyed. Her glasses fell off. He picked them up, laid them on a table and a moment later plucked them out of her overall pocket.

But the handkerchief was even more astounding. He rubbed his empty hands together and the next moment a handkerchief fluttered out of them.

She blinked in awe. "One of these days," he said, "I'll make some remarkable magic with an egg for you. Once an egg is broken, no one's supposed to be able to put it back together again but I can, princess. You wait and see."

"I'll tell my mommy," she said. "She says Humpty Dumpty was an egg and all the king's horses and all the king's men couldn't put him back together again. I'll tell her it's not true. I'll tell her you can."

There was no note of doubt in her tone. He was the magic grandfather. He could do anything.

"That's right," he said. "Tell her I have the gift of magic." He paused. "Maybe I'll have a chance to meet her and tell her myself."

Sarah glowed. "Are you going to stay a long time, Mr. Ferris?"

"Well, that depends on a lot of things."

"Like what?"

"Well, for one thing, on how long my daughter-in-law wants me to stay." He sent Mrs. Lane a mocking grin. "Why don't you ask her?"

"Oh." Sarah eyed her pleadingly. "Can he stay a long time? Can he stay —?" She broke off, her plea silenced by the frozen look on Mrs. Lane's face, and looked from one to the other uncertainly.

"We'll see," Mrs. Lane said in a neutral tone.

"That's the spirit, Etta." The old man nodded approvingly.

It was time for Sarah to leave. He helped her on with

her jacket and opened the back door for her. "Good-by, princess," he said.

"Good-by, Mr. Ferris." She gave him a brilliant smile, the small cloud cast by Mrs. Lane's attitude dispelled.

Mrs. Lane, reduced to the role of onlooker, felt a pang of jealousy. It was absurd, Sarah was a child and she a middle-aged woman. Their relationship might come under the all-embracing label of friendship but it was hardly one of equality. She shouldn't allow herself to feel jealous that Sarah was fascinated by the old man. Anyone who could do a few tricks would have the same effect on her or any other child.

Nevertheless, it was jealousy she felt watching him open the door for Sarah and being rewarded with a hero-worshiping smile.

At the last moment the little girl looked back and said, " 'Bye, Mrs. Lane."

"Good-by Sarah." Mrs. Lane felt a little better. Grateful, she thought wryly, for a crumb.

The old man closed the door, turned and said cheerly, "Well, that's my good deed for the day. Nothing like making a child happy. An old coat and a little sleight of hand are all that's needed. Coat may be rusty but I'm not, wouldn't you say?"

"No, you're not."

"Worked up an appetite playing magician." He looked at the clock over the sink. "Half-past eleven, Etta. I wouldn't mind an early lunch. That is"—he remembered to be scrupulous of his status as a guest—"if it wouldn't inconvenience you."

"No, it wouldn't." She could control her voice but not the hate and despair in her eyes as she looked at

43

him.

He met her gaze giving her back full measure of hatred in his look but not despair, just the sure gloating knowledge that he had the upper hand.

Sarah monopolized the conversation at dinner that night finding in her father a fresh audience for the wonders the old man had performed.

The others had already heard the story down to the last detail. The second time she interrupted Bobby's attempt to tell them about something that had happened at school that day he exclaimed in exasperation, "Crying out loud, Sarah, forget that old man for a minute, will you? Just one little minute? I'm so sick of hearing about him that—"

"—and said he's going to put the egg back together again after it's all broke," Sarah continued in serene disregard of her brother's protest. "Imagine doing that."

"That's not real magic," Bobby put in scornfully. "It's only a trick. There's no such thing as real magic anyways."

"There is so." Sarah thrust her lower lip out stubbornly.

"There is not. There's magicians doing tricks that's all. Only you're too little and dumb to know the difference. Your old magic grandfather couldn't fool me not one bit."

"You're jealous, Bobby, that's what." She glared at him. "You're jealous because you don't even know the magic grandfather and he'd never make magic for you if you did because you're too mean. You're so mean that—"

"All right," said their father. "That will do from both

44

of you."

The old man came into Sarah's conversation again at bedtime after she had said her prayers for her mother. They were alone in the bedroom, Amy being permitted to stay up half an hour longer on the grounds of seniority. This was a standing grievance of Sarah's but she wasn't thinking of it that night while her mother was tucking her in.

"Mommy," she said, "Mr. Ferris is a real magic grandfather, isn't he?"

"If he seems like one to you then that's what counts." Virginia Prince sat down on the side of the bed, leaned over to kiss her daughter's apple cheek and added, 'But no one has real magic, honey. Bobby's right about that. It's all just for fun."

"No," said Sarah sternly. "He's a real magic grandfather. You go to Mrs. Lane's house and meet him and then you'll know it's not just for fun." She hesitated. 'If he stays, I mean."

"Oh, he's mentioned leaving?" It was wrong, this picking for information, Virginia told herself, but anyone would be curious, how could they help it, the old man no one had ever heard of before, appearing from out of nowhere?

"He said it depends. Only—" Sarah sat up in bed with a troubled look.

"Only what, honey?"

"I don't think Mrs. Lane is glad he came. I don't think," her voice, uttering such heresy, dropped to a hushed note, "she likes Mr. Ferris. I don't think she wants him to stay. She looked so funny—"

"Well, what of it?" Virginia's tone was down to earth. "She doesn't have to like him just because she had him for a father-in-law years ago. She didn't invite him to visit her and doesn't have to be too pleased that he came as an uninvited guest."

Sarah looked shocked. "But, Mommy, he's — he's a magic grandfather. He does all those things and he laughs and tells jokes."

"That still doesn't mean Mrs. Lane has to be glad he came. Lie down and go to sleep now and stop fretting over it. Just remind yourself" — Virginia gave her a teasing smile — "that it's really none of our business how Mrs. Lane feels about Mr. Ferris or how he feels about her."

Sarah sighed and lay down. Her mother drew the covers up around her again and dropped a kiss on the tip of her nose. "Good night, honey," she said.

"G'night." The little girl's eyes followed her to the door. As the light went out she said anxiously, "Mommy, if Mrs. Lane doesn't want him to stay, couldn't we invite him to visit us?"

"We don't even know him," her mother pointed out, "and besides, we don't have a guest room."

"He could sleep on the sofa bed in the den."

"No, he couldn't — for the very good reason that he won't be invited to." Virginia's voice took on its crisp, that's-the-end-of-it note from which, experience had taught Sarah, there was no appeal.

She gave another sigh and subsided.

Later that evening, sitting with her husband in what was sometimes called the den and sometimes the family room, Virginia Prince's thoughts returned to the old man.

"He must have been a magician in his vaudeville days," she said expecting her husband to pick up her train of thought.

He was at his desk working on a bid for a house. He looked up and said, "Who? Oh, the old man up the street." Then after a pause to study the plumbing layout, "Lots of parlor magicians. What makes you think he was a pro?"

"Jane Kennedy mentioned it when she called me today. Said Dot Jensen heard it from Mrs. Bartlett."

"You women got little to do," said Ray Prince.

"Well, naturally people talk," Virginia defended herself. "How can they help thinking it strange, Mr. Ferris appearing so suddenly, when Mrs. Lane had never mentioned his existence to anyone?"

"Why should she? Her own business."

"Well, yes. Still, it's funny. No matter how much she keeps her affairs to herself you'd think that somewhere along the way she would have just mentioned—" Virginia broke off, picked up from a new angle. "Sarah doesn't think she likes him."

"Sarah's starting young," observed her father.

"Oh, not the way you mean," Virginia protested. "She wasn't being gossipy. She thinks the old man is wonderful and it bothers her that Mrs. Lane doesn't seem to share her feeling."

Silence from Ray Prince.

Undaunted, Virginia continued, "If they aren't on the best of terms and have been out of touch all these years it is strange, regardless of how you look at it, that he'd just arrive and plunk himself down on her. You wouldn't think he'd have the nerve."

"Mmm," said her husband not listening.

Chapter 4

Amy Prince, her tenth birthday near at hand, was above taking too much notice of what went on up the street, but Bobby wasn't. The day after Sarah rushed into the house ready to overwhelm her family with her tale of the egg crushed in a handkerchief and made whole again, Bobby went to the library and came home with a book on magic.

"Where's Sarah?" he demanded of his mother.

"She's playing over at Brenda's."

"Wait'll she gets home," he exulted, setting the book down on the kitchen table and turning the pages. "Wait'll I read her what it says here about the trick with the egg she thinks is so great. It tells how to do it. It says you sew two handkerchiefs together and leave a pocket. It says you take a pin and make a hole in each end of the egg and—"

"You're not to read that to Sarah," Virginia interrupted. "Let her enjoy the magic. Don't try to spoil it for her by telling her how it's done."

"But, Ma, she thinks it's real."

"She says she does but in her heart she knows better. She called it a magic game yesterday. That's the giveaway. But it makes it more fun for her to pretend it's real."

"Well, why doesn't she keep it to herself then? I don't come home and drive everyone nuts about games I've been playing." Bobby scowled at his mother. "I get sick of hearing about that old man."

"It's just a phase Sarah's going through," Virginia soothed. "Like you and riddles last fall. We all lived through that and we'll live through this."

The best way to live through it, she and her husband discovered, as the days became weeks and Sarah continued to bring home fresh stories of the miracles Dan Ferris performed, was to turn a deaf ear to her.

"Today," she would announce at the dinner table, "Mr. Ferris was raking the yard and I picked up an empty paper bag and when he opened it his watch was inside. It got in all by itself. It's a magic watch, he said." Or, "Today Mr. Ferris said hello to the china dog on the mantel and it said hello back." Or, "Today Mrs. Lane left her scarf on the chair while she went to get her coat and when she came back it was gone. I was right there and Mr. Ferris didn't touch it but it was under the seat cushion."

Bobby scoffed, Sarah's parents turned a deaf ear, Amy didn't hear it most of the time, being at the table in body eating her dinner, but in spirit deep in various episodes in the serial of her imaginary romance with a hall monitor boy in sixth grade whose name was Gary something unpronounceable and who was unaware of her existence.

"Mr. Ferris is paying Mrs. Lane quite a visit," Virginia remarked to her husband one night nearly three weeks after his arrival. "Sarah was wrong, it seems, about her not wanting him to stay."

Virginia met the old man herself a few days later when the bright April morning brought her outdoors to start spring gardening. Sarah saw him first, out for a walk, sauntering down the road toward them. When he came to their house he stopped out in front, greeted the little girl and introduced himself to her mother, sweeping off his hat with old-fashioned gallantry.

"Just out for a stroll before lunch," he said. "Beautiful day, Mrs. Prince. I see your crocuses are in bloom. They always look good after the winter, don't they?"

"Harbinger of spring," she said.

His white hair glistened in the sunlight. Freshly shaved, neat and clean in his dress—old men could be dirty and unkempt, she reflected—a smile lighting his thin face, he looked like a pleasant, friendly old man.

She smiled back at him. "We've been hearing a lot about you and your magic from Sarah, Mr. Ferris. It's kind of you to pay so much attention to her."

"My pleasure," he assured her and then added with a wink at the child, "That reminds me, what did I do with my handkerchief?" He rubbed his hands together and pulled it out of his hat. "Why, there it is."

Sarah giggled ecstatically, nudged her mother and said in a loud whisper, "See, Mommy, see."

Virginia laughed. "Yes indeed."

He put on his hat and put the handkerchief in his pocket. "Well, I must get back," he said. "Almost lunch time and my daughter-in-law likes me to be prompt. Then I have an errand downtown right after lunch."

He said good-by and turned back toward Mrs. Lane's, grinning to himself at the thought of how quickly the smile would vanish from Virginia Prince's face if she knew the nature of his errand downtown.

It had its roots in an incident that occurred a week after his arrival. Mrs. Lane was out doing her grocery shopping when the mail was delivered and as he brought it in the return address of Hall and Weaver, Investment Counselors, caught his eye. He steamed the envelope open and found a quarterly dividend check for $150.00 from National Chemical. The financial section of the morning paper listed the company at 85¼ paying an annual dividend of two dollars a share. He did rapid mental arithmetic that came out at three hundred shares worth well over twenty-five thousand dollars.

It wasn't the only stock Etta Lane owned. The other day, with her right there to take the mail from him he had noticed an envelope with the same investment firm's name on it; another dividend check, no doubt.

Etta, compared to him at least, was a rich woman. She had fallen into clover, marrying Lane after Jimmy's death, whereas all he had to show for the lean bitter years since was nine hundred dollars, slowly, laboriously saved, a dollar or two at a time, over three decades.

It was intolerable; the greatest injustice he had ever heard of.

But now their accounts would be balanced; Etta,

51

to blame for it all, would at last begin to pay for what she had done to him and Jimmy.

He was amiable at lunch that day. They ate breakfast and lunch in the kitchen, dinner in the dining room. The kitchen, facing southeast, was a cheerful room. Sunshine fell across the table through the south window, brightening Etta Lane's hair — very little touched up, he thought — and finding no flaws in her fair skin. It still looked satiny to the touch, her skin. He remembered it from all those years ago when he had made small excuses to cup her chin in his hand, pat her cheek, even, occasionally, plant a fatherly kiss on it. Satin skin then, satin skin now even though the bloom of youth was gone. Pushing fifty but could pass for ten years younger any time she chose. . . .

She was conscious of his veiled inspection but pretended not to notice it. It was just one more thing, not worth noticing, when her whole life had become a pretense since his arrival. It already seemed unbelievable that there had been a time, only a week ago, when she had been alone, mistress of her life, this man across the table a disagreeable but almost forgotten memory.

Part of the pretense, even when they were alone, was to behave as if they had a normal relationship. Not that she talked to him much but she listened when he rambled on about the old days, now cajoling, now needling her. She served him good meals and let him make himself useful in small ways, taking out the rubbish, cleaning up the yard, fixing the loose catch on the bathroom window.

You got used to anything, she thought that day,

watching him eat his lunch with hearty appetite. Anything, even his eyes sliding over her sometimes in a way that set her nerves on edge. But since she had first caught him looking at her like that she had hunted up the key to her bedroom door and started locking it at night.

When lunch was over she rose to clear the table but he made a restraining gesture and said, "Wait a minute, Etta. Couple of things I want to talk to you about."

"What?" She sat down again.

His eyes narrowed in anger. "Couldn't you show a little politeness and call me by name once in a while? Don't think I haven't noticed, Etta, how you've been avoiding it ever since I got here. It's not hard to say. It's Dan, D-a-n. Nothing hard about that, is there?"

(But Jimmy calls you Pa, she'd said in the old days. Shouldn't I? He had laughed and pinched her cheek. I'd rather Dan. I'm not the fatherly type.)

So he had become Dan to her. But now it was different. She couldn't bring herself to address him by name.

It was pointless, though, to antagonize him unnecessarily.

"No — Dan," she replied.

"That's better." He nodded and hunched forward in his chair putting his elbows on the table. "Now, about my visit here: I know you'd rather have my room than my company but there's the question of money, Etta girl. I couldn't say this outside but here in the bosom of the family, so to speak, I'll come right out and say I'm pretty strapped at the present

53

time and have no better prospects for the future."

Relife flooded her. It was all a question of money. She would give it to him and he would go, leaving her free to pick up her life again where he had disrupted it.

"I told you the night you came that I'd give you money," she said.

"Ah yes. But from the way you spoke"—he wrinkled his forehead in disdain—"you meant a few hundreds, a mere flea bite, Etta."

So it was to be a bargaining session. She made a quick review of her resources in ready cash; about three thousand in savings and close to the same amount in her checking account. Start small and work up to offering him most of it.

"I might be able to raise a little more," she said. "Perhaps fifteen hundred."

He shook his head. "I'm thinking of a real nest egg, not something you could raise overnight. Oh, I'll take that much for a down payment, but my true aim, Etta, is a backlog for my old age."

He paused and then continued, "I come of a long-lived family, you know, and if Jimmy hadn't been cut off in the flower of his youth he'd probably have lived to a ripe old age too. So I'm thinking in terms of twenty-five to thirty thousand Etta."

"Twenty-five to thirty—?" She eyed him in disbelief. "Why, that's—"

"Call it a settlement, the kind insurance companies make," he inserted sharply. "Twenty-five to thirty thousand for Jimmy's life. Long overdue and cheap at the price."

"Impossible," she exclaimed. "I couldn't get by

myself if I gave you that much of my capital. Ed's capital. It came from him, it has nothing to do with Jimmy. It's—"

"There's your National Chemical stock," he said softly. "I'd settle for that, Etta. Sell it, give me the money and I'll be on my way and you'll never hear from me again."

"You opened my mail." She couldn't work up indignation over what was, after all, only a small part of the crushing whole.

"Just trying to get a picture of your financial situation."

"I couldn't give you all that. It's my cushion, my margin beyond the necessities." She sprang to her feet, too wrought up to sit at the table with him, and began to clear away the dishes.

"You've had too much cushion in your life, Etta, and I've had too little. It's time things were evened up a bit, wouldn't you say?"

His tone was still soft; with her back turned to him at the sink she did not see the malignant gaze he fixed on her.

No use arguing with him about Jimmy's death. No use? Rinsing and stacking the dishes she admitted to herself that she didn't dare, not knowing how he would react after heaping all the blame on her since the day it happened.

He couldn't face the part he had played in it himself; she must never let him goad her into making accusations of her own.

When she held her silence he continued, "Of course, like I told you the day I came, you've got a choice: you can hang on to your money and let me

55

tell people how Jimmy died. You couldn't live it down here, though, so you'd have to pull up stakes and start over again somewhere else. Not as easy to do as when you were young, Etta, and not as safe, because I'd bide my time until you were settled and then tell my story again."

He paused. "I'm making you a fair and square offer, girl, to buy my silence. If you don't accept it I'll keep on your trail till one of us is in our grave."

She did not answer him for a moment, not wanting to scream at him or burst into tears. At last she said in a low careful tone, "Greg Weaver, who was a friend of my husband's, handles my investments. They're in what brokers call a street name so that he can buy and sell more easily. I couldn't possibly ask him to sell all my National Chemical. He'd want to know why. Should I say you're blackmailing me?"

"Oh." The old man thought this over. "It'll have to be piecemeal, I guess. Have him sell a third of it now and tell him you want some extra cash or you're going to invest it in real estate or whatever you please. Turn the money over to me and then in another couple of months sell some more of it. Or some other stock if you'd rather."

She walked over to the table eying him coldly but with veiled hope. "If I do that, sell a third of it now, will you leave and let me send on the rest?"

He shook his head. "I'll leave when I get it all, every cent that's due me. Not before, Etta. Not an hour, not a minute before."

She thought wildly of going to Greg Weaver with the truth, telling him to sell it all and let her pay off the old man. Then a mental picture of Weaver flashed through her mind, sitting at his desk, upright, self-contained, a man of impeccable background who had never been mixed up in anything questionable in his life. Ed's friend. Ed had been just like him. She had never told Ed her past and she could never tell it to Weaver.

She had to get out of this trap alone.

She began to think of possible reasons she could give for selling the first hundred shares of National Chemical.

In the end she told Weaver that through a friend in Ohio she was going to invest the money in land. He offered to have the project investigated for her and turned stiff with disapproval when she refused, but had to agree to sell the stock.

The check had come from him in the morning's mail. While the old man was out for his walk she took it to her bank saying she wanted it in cash despite the teller's protest that it was too much money to carry around.

It was an embarrassing moment but at noon she was home turning the money over to Dan Ferris trying to get a receipt for it and being refused.

There were two banks in Harrington. The errand the old man mentioned to Virginia Prince that morning took him to the savings bank to open an account with a deposit of $8200.00.

He left the house in a jaunty mood, thinking of the good start he was making and that while he continued to live free off Etta, waiting for her to settle his claim in full, he could build up his account a little more every month out of his social security check.

A penny saved was a penny earned. A man's best friend was his pocketbook.

With these pleasant reflections to occupy his mind he stepped out briskly on his way to the bank.

Etta Lane stood at the front window and watched him go. Nodding and smiling at a neighbor up the street, he did not look like the evil old man he was, battening off the sins of her youth. But then, she had never given a thought before to what a blackmailer should look like.

She had no real hope of getting rid of him. He would leave temporarily when she met his present demands but he would be back. He would be fastened around her neck as long as he lived just as he had once, in a different sort of way, been fastened around Jimmy's.

She had forgotten how much she had hated him in those days; but now that hatred had come back, increased a thousandfold.

Chapter 5

Mrs. Lane did not know the old man had sent for his trunk until the Railway Express Company truck stopped in front of the house two weeks later and the driver's helper rang the doorbell to ask where she wanted the trunk put.

Before she got past saying What trunk? Dan Ferris bounced down the stairs and took charge.

"It's to go upstairs in my room," he said. "Just bring it in and I'll show you the way."

She stood on the porch, the situation taken out of her hands, watching them wrestle the wardrobe trunk out of the truck, big old black object, twice as shabby as she remembered it, looking not unlike a coffin in the spring sunlight. In a sense, it was a coffin, this relic of the past, repository of vanished dreams, days brighter in retrospect than in reality. God alone knew how many miles it had traveled with its owner in the old days or what mementos of them it contained. God alone knew how long it had been moldering in some warehouse awaiting the day when he would have the money to redeem it and a place to keep it. Now, it seemed, he thought that day had come.

Her heart sank watching the men ease it through the front door and up the stairs, Dan Ferris excitedly leading the way, telling them to take care. Then she stiffened. He needn't think he could find free storage for it here. She would not have it, a seal of permanence stamped on his re-entry into her life. When she got the rest of his money together she would tell him the trunk had to leave with him or she would have it taken to the dump.

When the expressmen left she expected him to call her upstairs while he opened it. But he shut himself up in his room with it and did not appear again until dinnertime.

It wasn't mentioned at table. He made no reference to it and Etta Lane asked no questions since it was her practice to ask him nothing about his private affairs and to volunteer no information about her own. Their talk was limited to news items, local events, the weather. The closest they came to having a common bond was the pleasure they both took in Sarah Prince's company.

The old man confined his conversation to how warm the day had been.

"Time to take down the storm windows and get the screens up," he said. "Do you hire someone to do it, Etta?"

"The boy up the street."

"No need for it this year. I'll start on them tomorrow." His face broke into a grin. "Wouldn't want to see you spending money for nothing, girl."

She held back the retort about where her money was going that came inevitably into her mind. Why not let him take care of the windows? she thought

Let him save her a few dollars, earn a little of his keep.

Yesterday he had cleaned the garage. He had time on his hands for such chores but he was probably the most expensive handyman anyone had ever employed.

The trunk stood against the wall near his bureau when she went into his room the next morning to dust and make the bed. As she looked at it the thought came back that it looked like a tall black upended coffin.

On the bureau was another object from the past, a heavy bronze statue of Thespis that had weighed down his suitcase from one town to the next. His good luck piece, he called it, given to him by some friend in his early days of vaudeville.

She picked it up, set it down. She had forgotten it existed.

The old man was still downstairs reading the paper. She yielded to curiosity and tried to open the trunk. It was locked.

Had he taken anything else out of it? She looked in his closet. Nothing in it that hadn't been there since he first arrived.

In the top drawer of the bureau she found a photograph they had used in their billing. The Four Ferrises, it said, Dan, Jimmy, Ella and Etta. There they were, faded, old-fashioned looking, she and Ella in identical beaded evening dresses, all with bright, artificial smiles pasted on their faces, all but Ella trying to look famous and successful and somehow looking only forlorn, a little tawdry.

Those wretched dresses, she thought; the beads

kept coming off them at the cleaner's and she had to keep sewing them on.

Shabby little dressing rooms with naked bulbs hanging from the ceiling, herself sewing with one eye on the clock, the old man — middle-aged then — hovering in the doorway, drifting into the room and finding some excuse to touch her, no matter how often she drew back from it. This she remembered well and Jimmy's never noticing it, never admitting that his father could do wrong, least of all to him.

Poor Jimmy. Doggedly cheerful, always looking on the bright side of things, always ready with an optimistic cliché, never say die, every cloud has a silver lining, tomorrow will be better.

Poor Jimmy. Eager, facile, shallow; quick, until the last night of his life, to avoid showdowns, unpleasantness of any sort.

Poor Jimmy. Living by clichés. Can't let the old man down — when she pleaded with him to break away from the act — vaudeville's his whole life. A shrug when she said, But it's not ours, we're young, we can make a fresh start, his arm around her, his voice coaxing. Let's just stick it out a little longer, Etta, just until Pa himself admits vaudeville's a dead duck, then we'll strike out on our own.

He'll never admit it, she said.

He'll have to, said Jimmy.

But he never had.

Poor Jimmy. Deeply wronged by his father, deeply wronged by her, his wife.

She studied his face in the picture. Theater face. Bright smile, bright emptiness.

She had no picture of him. She had forgotten

what he looked like, the young man dead so many years.

How many? Almost twenty-seven, wasn't it? Yes, toward the end of June—or was it early July?

It seemed sad that she couldn't remember the date. Perhaps not though. Perhaps it just meant that she had rebuilt her life so well that there was no need to mark the anniversaries of sorrows past.

Poor Jimmy. Poor Etta Owens, the naive girl of thirty years ago, clerking in her father's drugstore, dazzled by the young actor, too ready to dream of a glamorous life with him.

All that was left of that girl and boy were memories she did not often take out like this to examine.

No, there was one thing more. There was the old man downstairs, Jimmy's legacy to her, his blackmailing father.

Was there some rightness, some expiation of guilt in that? She didn't know.

She put the picture back into the drawer.

While she was making the old man's bed, she heard voices below, Sarah's, then the old man's. They came upstairs into the room together.

"Hi, Mrs. Lane," said the little girl.

"Good morning, Sarah. How are you today?"

"Good." Sarah's gaze was already fixed on the trunk. "What's that?"

"My trunk," said Dan Ferris from the doorway.

She crossed the room and touched it tentatively. "Is it a magic trunk?"

"Well, it has certain magic properties."

"Can I see inside?"

"I'm afraid it's locked."

She turned to look at him. "But you can open it, can't you?"

"If I did, princess, it might lose its magic. Magic is secret stuff, you know."

"But I want to see inside," Sarah persisted.

"Well, you can't, princess, and that's that." He grinned to soften his refusal and glanced at Etta who was smoothing out the bedspread.

"Nobody," he said speaking to her, not the child, "will see what's in the trunk until I decide the time is right—if I ever do." He did a few tap steps and sang, "Yes, sir, the trunk's my baby, yes, sir, don't mean maybe—"

Sarah's pout, the outthrust lower lip that signaled her displeasure, vanished in laughter.

"Let's go downstairs now and you can help me with the storm windows," the old man said holding out his hand to her.

They went downstairs. Mrs. Lane, when she finished tidying his room, shifted the trunk slightly. It was heavy, yes, but with no great excess of weight.

What did he have in it so precious that it had to be locked up? For all the jesting note he struck, he had served warning on her that the trunk was not to be opened until he decided the time was right—if he ever did.

Right for what?

It made her nervous, tall black upended coffin. Pandora's box, Bluebeard's chamber . . .

What melodramatic thoughts she was having.

She went across the hall to her room. She would never ask what was in the trunk. She would never ask the old man anything.

64

He took down the storm windows, washed and stored them away, the downstairs ones in the garage, the upstairs ones in the attic. He hung the screens, taking his time, a few each day, spreading the task out over a week.

It was May, the buds on the apple tree in the yard were swelling before the windows were finished. Then he turned his attention to spading flowerbeds and borders for planting.

There was no doubt that he had his uses. Fertilizing and planting was the next of his self-assigned chores.

The day this was finished he went upstairs to take a bath as soon as he came into the house. He was very clean in his person, you had to grant him that, Etta Lane reflected, hearing the water run overhead while she was getting dinner. Even an evil old man like him had to have some good points and she had to keep them in mind to preserve balance in the peculiar neutral relationship that had developed between them. Like two armed camps they had declared a truce, delicate, precarious but somehow maintained since she had paid her first installment of blackmail.

Next week, with a decent interval elapsed, she would see Greg Weaver about selling another block of National Chemical. He was going to make an even bigger fuss this time. She would sound him out on when he was making his annual trip to California—it was usually the latter part of June—and sell the last of National Chemical while he was away. In other words, it was going to take her another six weeks or so to pay off the old man and get rid of him; and ten years, probably, to recoup what he was costing her—unless, in the meantime, he came back for more.

If he did, she would have to go to the police. Disgrace was better than beggary.

But for the present, there was the truce to maintain.

Dan Ferris breeched it almost immediately. He came downstairs out into the kitchen while she was taking the rib roast out of the oven, sniffed appreciatively and said, "My, that smells good. You've become quite a cook, Etta girl."

He walked over to her as he spoke and slipped his arm around her waist from behind. "Quite a cook," he repeated.

She set the roast down, flung off his arm and whirled around to face him.

"Don't ever do that again," she said. "Don't ever dare touch me. It's no part of our bargain."

"Why—" he retreated a step. "Just a friendly gesture. Didn't mean a thing."

"Didn't it? You used to paw me like that in the old days every chance you got. I wasn't all that green not to notice it."

She picked up the carving knife, her face white with anger, her eyes blue fire. "See that you keep your hands to yourself from now on," she said.

"You were crazy if you ever had thoughts like that," he muttered retreating another step. "After all, a little affection—I was your father-in-law—"

"Yes, you were. You took advantage, knowing I couldn't make an issue of it. But just remember that now it's different."

"If that's the way you want it." He was back in the hall doorway.

"That's exactly the way I want it and the way it's going to be. The paper's come. It's in the living room. I'll call you when dinner's ready."

He vanished. She turned back to the stove. Her hand shook holding the knife. She laid it down.

She wouldn't wait until next week to arrange for the second installment of the money. She would see Greg Weaver tomorrow. No, tomorrow was Saturday. It would have to be Monday.

It was too bad that she couldn't tell him to sell all of her National Chemical and get the whole thing over with but she didn't dare. She shrank, as it was, from the prospect of telling him to sell another hundred shares.

She would have to put up with the old man a little longer. But at least, in one sense, she had put him in his place.

Chapter 6

Dan Ferris kept out of her way most of the weekend, particularly Sunday when it rained. He shut himself in his room that day and although Mrs. Lane heard him moving around occasionally, there were intervals of silence that made her wonder how he managed to occupy himself.

In midafternoon a married couple, the Snyders, dropped in, accompanied by Mrs. Snyder's brother who had come over from a nearby town to spend the day.

The Snyders thought Dan Ferris was good company and asked for him as soon as they were settled in the living room. He came downstairs, greeted them cheerily and was introduced to Mrs. Synder's brother who was also meeting Mrs. Lane for the first time.

His name was John Frear. He was an attractive man in his early fifties, a widower since last fall and, it developed, a man of some substance, sales manager of a manufacturing concern.

Dan Ferris kept a thoughtful eye on him while acting as host, making drinks for everyone and entertaining them with reminiscences of his vaudeville days. He did not miss the signs of interest that Frear showed in Etta Lane who looked youthfully pretty that afternoon in a dark cotton dress and high heeled pumps that displayed her nice legs to advantage.

When the talk turned to duplicate bridge Frear said

he sometimes played it and it was presently arranged that Mrs. Lane and he would play together Friday evening in the weekly game at the Harrington Community Center.

There was no way for him to know as he shook hands with the old man on leaving, telling him how much he'd enjoyed his stories, that he had just fashioned another club to be held over Etta Lane's head.

But she knew. Standing beside the old man in the doorway she saw the look of satisfaction on his face and had no trouble reading his mind.

Nevertheless, she felt a small glow of pleasure at the prospect of seeing John Frear again. He was the most eligible male she had met in eighteen months of widowhood. They did not grow on bushes for women of fifty.

The rain had stopped within the past half hour and as their callers drove away the sun broke through the thinning clouds. Dan Ferris, looking up at the sky, gave it a nod of approval as if he were responsible for the brighter weather and said, "Guess I'll take a little walk. Fresh air will do me good. Anything you need from downtown, Etta?"

"No, nothing at all. I'll start dinner. It'll be ready in about an hour."

"I'll be back." He went down the porch steps and out to the road heading toward the center. She lingered a moment in the doorway noticing his springy gait. He had the walk of a man years younger; he had the good health of such a man. He would live for years yet.

She left the door open to the late afternoon sunshine as she went upstairs to her room. She would have said she went up for no particular reason but there was one. She wanted to look at herself in the full-length mirror

69

on her closet door. She stood in front of it trying to see herself through Frear's eyes. Her face wore a faint becoming flush. Her blonde hair looked perfectly natural, as well it should, she thought, considering the outrageous price she paid her hairdresser for a touch-up job. But it was worth the money.

She ran a comb through it smiling the secret smile of a woman pleased with her appearance. She did look her best today and John Frear had shown interest in her.

She, in turn, felt attracted to him. He reminded her a little of Ed. Not in looks, but he had the same quiet easy manner.

She wasn't thinking of the old man when she came out of her room but his closed door across the hall caught her eye. It usually stood open when he wasn't in his room.

She found herself opening it. The bed was on her left. Lying on it was a beaded red chiffon dress. She caught her breath. It looked like . . .

She walked over to it and picked it up. It was the dress she had worn in the act years ago, the one she was wearing in the picture.

She spread it out for a closer look. Dingy, faded, half the crystal beads gone or hanging by a thread, it was her dress. Or it was Ella's, identical even to size.

No, it was hers. There was her name tape sewed in nearly thirty years ago.

She put the dress down and stood looking at it blankly. Why had the old man kept it all these years? Why?

She heard him just then, or rather, heard hasty footsteps on the porch, and darted out of the room closing the door quietly after her. She had just time to shut herself into her own room before he came running upstairs.

Then there was no sound for a moment. She could sense, almost see him eying her door before he went into his, slamming the door behind him.

He'd had the dress out, she thought, when she called him downstairs earlier. Always eager for company, an audience for his stories, he hadn't stopped to put the dress away before he made his appearance. By the time the Snyders and John Frear left, he had forgotten it was out of the trunk and hadn't thought of it again until after he had set out for his walk. Then he had come rushing back to put it away.

She sat down at her dressing table. The flush of a few minutes ago was gone from her face. She was pale, her eyes looking wide and dark against her pallor. She felt chilled by her discovery.

That old rag of a dress—why had he kept it all these years?

Not as a memento of her in the act, no, not that. He had hated her in the end. He would have kept nothing of hers for that reason or any normal reason that she could think of.

But he had kept it and took it out from time to time, it seemed.

What else did he have locked away in the trunk? The red slippers she'd worn with the dress?—the ribbon she'd worn in her hair when they did their little girl and her daddy routine?—the ruffled blue dress and Mary Janes that went with it? Did he, in some sort of voodoo rite, stick pins in the costumes as a symbol or substitute for her?

71

Even worse, did the dress represent some form of fetishism?

She shivered at the thought. He hated her and yet . . .

"Something about you, Etta, that gets under a man's skin," he'd said in the old days making it a joke but meaning it.

He hated her but was physically attracted to her. That was what he'd meant then. She didn't know if it was still true or what the dress meant to him now.

She would have to get him out of the house immediately, sell the rest of her National Chemical tomorrow to do it. Never mind what Greg Weaver said or thought. Her overriding concern was to get rid of the old man.

He knocked on her door. "You in there, Etta?"

"Yes, just freshening up." She got to her feet, crossed the room and opened the door.

It was an effort to speak to him. "That was a short walk," she said.

"Forgot my wallet." His eyes searched her face for some clue that would tell him she had seen the dress.

She looked back at him calmly. "Well, I'm going downstairs and start dinner now."

He looked at her again, nodded and went down ahead of her and out of the house.

She did not need to look into his room to know that the dress was no longer on the bed.

All she could think of was that tomorrow she would sell the stock. In another few days she would have the money and see the last of him.

She could hardly wait.

Chapter 7

But it was only a dream of freedom.

He listened impassively at the dinner table an hour later when she told him she was going to try to get all his money together by the end of the week.

"That is, unless the check takes a day or two longer," she added. "Even if it does, Dan"—might as well be placatory and call him by name—"you can start making plans to leave somewhere around that time."

He shook his head, still impassive, showing nothing of gratification. He speared the last piece of meat on his plate, chewed and swallowed it.

She waited on tenterhooks for him to speak.

He raised his napkin to his lips and said, "Very good dinner for Jenny the spinner—that's a silly little rhyme I learned as a kid. Now how did the rest of it go? Something about ducks in a mill pond all in a flutter."

He was tormenting her deliberately. "What's for dessert?" he inquired.

She couldn't stand it. "Dan—"

The sly grin that so irritated her crossed his face. "Very quick to call me by name, aren't you, when you want something? Like now, when you're in a great hurry to get rid of me." Another headshake. "You will, Etta, you will, but not as quick as would suit you."

"We made a bargain and as soon as I've kept my part of it you must keep yours." She heard her voice rise in anger and made an effort to control it. "In common decency," she appended on a lower note.

"Yes, you're right about that, Etta girl. And I will keep it. Get the money and I'll go like I said but not immediately." He paused, repeated himself, "Not immediately. Decoration Day is week after next so let's say I'll leave right after the Fourth of July. You can put up with me that much longer, Etta. Time flies between those two holidays."

"No," she said. "You've got to live up to your bargain and leave as soon as I get your money together." She rose to clear the table. "I don't want you in my house a minute longer than I can help."

"You don't have a choice," he said as she carried plates out to the kitchen. "You can't help having me a few weeks more so why not make the best of it?"

She turned back to face him. "You don't care about the bird in the hand? What if something happened to me during those weeks? You'd be out all that money."

The sliding glance she abhorred went over her. "You look good and healthy. You drive careful and Mr. Frear," the sly grin again, "looks like a careful driver too. I'll take my chances that you'll be around to pay off and that I'll be around to collect. I figure all I got to worry about is to watch out crossing streets. Yes, that's about all."

His voice took on a meditative note. "Most people in my position, I guess, worry about the source of their money turning on them but I don't feel I have that problem Etta. Because if, for instance, you dropped some arsenic in my coffee, you'd defeat your own purpose. Just the publicity, whether you were accused of murder or not, would bring out who I was and the whole story about Jimmy."

"Dear God, I can't stand the sight of you!" The cry burst from her lips.

"I feel exactly the same way about you," he replied icily.

"Then take your money and go!" She was almost shouting at him.

His icy calm held. "I'll go when I said I would, right after the Fourth. In fact, I'll make a bus reservation for July the fifth. That is, if you'll give me the money two or three days ahead so I can put it in my bank account and arrange for some travelers checks."

"But why not do all that and leave by Memorial Day?" she demanded.

"Because I don't want to," he said with nothing at all in his voice. "Because I'd rather stay a few weeks longer. Round things out, so to speak."

Helpless fury swept across her face. "What things? What could there possibly be for you to round out here?"

"Things," he said with inexorable quiet. "Just things."

She had a thought. "The bank interest. You put the money you already got from me in the savings bank, didn't you?"

"Yes."

"And they pay interest the first of July. Is that what you mean about rounding things out?"

"The interest?" His tone turned reflective. "Why, yes, I guess you could put it like that. The interest."

He would say no more and would not budge from his position.

She retreated to the kitchen at last, served dessert—ridiculous to be serving dessert to this evil old man as if he were just any guest in her house—but could not touch it herself.

He ate his with good appetite and drank two cups of coffee.

They were both silent during this interval. The two armed camps they represented had broken the truce between them. It would take time to patch it up again.

Sarah arrived while they were still at the table. She could not reach the bell and banged on the back door as was her custom until told to come in.

"I can't find my red ball," she announced without preliminaries from the kitchen. "Did I leave it here, Mrs. Lane?"

"I don't know but I'll help you look," she replied, glad to leave the table.

They couldn't find the red ball.

"Maybe you left it somewhere in the yard," the old man suggested. "I'll help you look out there."

"Couldn't you find it by magic?" Sarah asked hopefully.

He laughed and took her hand. "Let's see if we can't find it by looking."

They went outside together, Sarah serenely confident he would find her ball, he noncommittal. They made a pleasant sight, the smiling old man and the little girl skipping along beside him, pushing her unmanageable hair back off her forehead every moment or two.

It was still broad daylight. Through the window over the sink Mrs. Lane watched them moving around the yard, the sun falling on Sarah's untidy fair head and the old man's neat white head with impartial beneficence.

No one would believe her, she thought frantically as she stacked the dishes in the dishwasher, if she told them what a terrible person he was. Sometimes, looking at him, she couldn't believe it herself.

How she hated him. He was the only person she had ever really hated in her life. She had hated him in the old days and far more now. She had forgotten what the feeling was like in the time between.

But she had never got the better of him then or now. Bafflement and helplessness fed her hatred.

The ball was found in the back of the garage, Sarah dancing into the house ahead of Dan Ferris with the happy tidings. "But it wasn't magic," she added. "It was just there and I saw it first."

"Oh, is it magic you want?" The old man stepped across the threshold. "Get the pack of cards in the living room drawer, princess, and I'll show you some."

She knew which drawer and ran to get them.

"Pick one," he said holding out the pack to her.

She picked one and showed it to Mrs. Lane. "Is that a three?" she asked in a loud whisper.

77

"Yes, it's the three of hearts."

Sarah handed it back and waited looking at him expectantly over the rims of her glasses.

He got a goblet from the cupboard, put the pack into it and made passes over it with both hands. The three of hearts rose from the goblet and seemed to hang in the air.

Sarah rolled on the floor in ecstasy.

There never was anyone in the whole world like the magic grandfather, she told her mother going to bed that night.

He walked her home, was invited in and had a highball with her parents making himself so agreeable that they were bound to say what a nice old man he was after he left.

Etta Lane tried to read while he was gone but couldn't sit still long enough. She got up from her chair and roamed the house, every nerve in her body jumping. She looked at her desk calendar. Six weeks and six days to July 5 — how could she get through them?

Not by letting her hatred of the old man rule her. That would do more injury to herself than to him.

Think of the positive side. Today was virtually over. Tomorrow there would be only forty-seven days left.

She picked up a pencil and drew a faint line through today, May 18.

Perhaps when she had the money ready for him she wouldn't have to mark off any more days. Perhaps the offer to write a check immediately would loom larger for him than his talk of rounding things out or, in other words, collecting the interest on the money he'd already put in the bank.

That was what he had meant, wasn't it? There was nothing else it could be. If she offered to check with the bank on how much the interest would come to and make it up herself would he go then?

She could at least suggest it.

Her restlessness took her upstairs and presently into the old man's room to stand and stare at the trunk and wonder again what was in it.

It had a stout lock. She could not open it. She had long since tried every key in the house on it but none of them worked.

Dusk had set in. In the dim light the trunk looked more than ever like a coffin but she made no move toward the light switch. She didn't want the old man, on his way back from the Princes', to see a light in his room.

He carried the key to the trunk on his person. She had never laid eyes on it and knew she never would. Unless he forgot to lock it some day, she had no prospect of finding out what other souvenirs of the past he had kept along with her red dress.

Just thinking of the dress made her desperate to get him out of the house.

If he would let her pay him off now and go away taking the trunk with him she would feel as if she had a new start in life.

She broached the subject as soon as he got back from the Princes'.

"I'll call the bank tomorrow and find out how much interest would be due the first of July and make it up to you," she said.

She stopped him in the hall on his way up to his

room. He leaned against the newel post and gave her a sidewise look.

"Don't bother," he said. "I'm leaving July 5 and not one day earlier."

"But why not? If I give you the interest money what's to keep you from—?"

"You're the one's talking about that," he interrupted her. "I never mentioned it myself. I said I was staying to round things out."

"But what do you mean by it? What has to be rounded out?"

"Things," he answered. "Just things."

It was a replay of their earlier conversation.

"I can't imagine what you're talking about."

"Can't you? Well, like I said, things."

He went up to his room calling good night from the top of the stairs.

All that was left for her to do was to go and look bleakly at her desk calendar.

Chapter 8

Day after day Etta Lane crossed off the date and turned the page to a new day. June 1 was a particular victory; then she could say to herself, Next month he'll be gone. June 5 she could say, A month from today he'll be gone, I'll have my house to myself again.

It became four weeks, three weeks, two weeks. . . .

Braving Greg Weaver's disapproval, she sold the rest of her National Chemical, received payment and deposited it in her checking account ready to write a check for the old man.

Their truce had been re-established; delicately balanced out for her, at least, easier to keep as she marked off the days that brought his departure nearer.

She did not allow herself to dwell on what a considerable portion of her money she would soon be giving away. She thought more often about John Frear, the new interest and hope he had brought into her life.

He had taken her out several times, to duplicate bridge games, to dinner, to summer theater and then, just before he was to leave on a business trip, to a Sunday night cookout at the Snyders'.

She had bought two new dresses since she met him.

Dan Ferris looked on with cynical interest, assigning himself the role of father waving paternal good-bys from the front porch.

Frear tended to like him or at least to regard him with

amused tolerance.

"Real fond of you, isn't he?" he remarked the night of the cookout when the old man followed her out to the car with a sweater in case the evening turned chilly. "Doesn't seem to be much trouble. Lively too. Company for you around the house."

"Yes," she said and felt a lump of tears she could not shed rise in her throat. "Company for me."

She found it an effort to talk during the drive to the Snyders'. Frear's casually friendly view of the old man whose victim she was created a gap between them almost as wide as if they spoke different languages. She had never felt more alone.

Several people at the cookout asked how her father-in-law was, smiling when they brought up his name, liking him, it seemed, in much the same way that Frear did.

She tried to cheer herself with the thought that a week from Saturday he would be gone and brightened further when the idea came that she might then have a cookout of her own, symbol of release from her thralldom. She had done no entertaining since the old man's arrival.

She mentioned it to Frear on the way home when he suggested that they plan something to celebrate his return from his trip that would take him out to the Coast for two weeks.

"Well, I've been thinking of having a cookout," she said. "Why don't I have it that night?"

He smiled. "Welcome home cookout?"

"Yes, that's a good name for it."

"Then I want engraved invitations sent out. You are cordially invited to attend a welcome home cookout in honor of Mr. John Frear, Tuesday evening, July 8 — "

She laughed, suddenly feeling more lighthearted than she had the whole evening.

At the front door he bent and kissed her on the cheek as they said good night.

She skimmed up the stairs like a girl.

He phoned her Monday night to say good-by. As she hung up she thought how much she liked him and then that it wouldn't be hard to learn to love him.

Dan Ferris, reading the newspaper, glanced up from it and caught her eye.

"Looks like Frear's getting sweet on you," he said. "Off with the old love, on with the new, eh?"

Her pleasure in Frear's call vanished.

"You're talking nonsense," she said coldly.

"I don't think so. You should see yourself, bright and chipper as a girl. You'll be getting married again. Never mind Jimmy, never mind your second husband, that's your style. You always manage to land in clover, don't you? Frear's got money, you can smell it off him."

"Shut up," she said and walked out of the room.

A week later she paid off the old man. National Chemical had gone up since her first payment of blackmail. She wrote him a check for seventeen thousand dollars that Tuesday morning and watched him set out for the bank with it.

On his way home he stopped at the bus station and bought a ticket to New York.

Having him show it to her dulled the edge of her resentment over the check she had written.

"What are you planning to do about your trunk?" he asked.

"Oh, I'll call Railway Express and have them pick i up next week. They can hold it in Miami until I ge there."

She no longer cared what he had in it. The shock o seeing her dress had worn off and now all that mattere was to have him remove himself and his trunk from he house.

Nevertheless, she tried shifting it again while she wa in the old man's room the next morning. It seemed n heavier or lighter than it had ever been. The old ma hadn't added or removed anything from it since it ha been restored to him.

She spun around at a chuckle from the doorway. H stood there eying her maliciously.

"Nose bothering you?" he said.

She regained her poise. "No, I'm just moving it s that I can dry mop the floor."

"Zatso?" he said in disbelief and then, rocking bac and forth on his heels, "Maybe I'll show you what's i the trunk before I leave, Etta. Maybe. It depends o you."

"I wouldn't be interested," she said briefly.

"I think you would." An undertone of ferocity can into his voice. "Yes, I think you would."

She made no reply but began to dust the burea When she looked up the doorway was empty.

Downstairs again, she went outdoors and cast a cri ical eye over the yard. Dan Ferris still cut the grass b since the beginning of hot weather no longer took ca of the borders and flowerbeds. He had to look aft himself at his age, he said. He didn't want to overexer bring on a stroke.

She had refrained from saying that nothing wou

suit her better.

She was far behind on weeding and might as well put in an hour at it before the sun got too hot. It would take her days to get the yard back in shape and she wanted it to look its best for her cookout. Also, she'd better begin to give some thought to what people she would invite. Not too many. Three or four couples beside John Frear and herself would be enough. The Snyders, of course. . . .

She got out the gardening tools and set to work on the front border.

The old man emerged from the house and stood on the porch watching her.

She was wearing shorts. She became conscious of his gaze resting on her bare legs and tucked them under her.

"You've got a lot more modest, Etta, than you used to be," he said sardonically and when she ignored the taunt descended the steps jingling change in his pocket.

"I'm going to take a walk downtown. Need anything?"

He took lots of walks. Walking was good for the health.

Her hands trembled with the force of her hatred of him. She yanked a weed out of the ground.

"Nothing at all," she said.

He was in no hurry. "I was just thinking that I'll be gone before your birthday comes around next week," he said. "Must get you something before I leave."

She turned a level glance on him. "Don't bother. All I want from you is for you to go away and never come back."

85

His mild look hardened. "Don't worry about that," he said. "I have no more use for you than you have for me."

"Then just stay away from me. Because if you ever do come back"—she pointed the trowel at him for emphasis—"I'll go straight to the police. My bank statements put side by side with yours will show that you've blackmailed me. It wasn't too smart of you to put the money in the bank here."

He was unmoved by her threat. "Isn't the fact that I did it proof that I won't be back for more?" His sly grin came. "But just out of curiosity, Etta—if I came back and by that time you were Mrs. John Frear, do you think you'd be so brave about the police?"

"Yes," she said through her teeth. "Yes, I would."

"I wonder," he said. "I just wonder . . ."

He sauntered out of the yard and turned toward downtown.

Her eyes followed him. It had been an unpleasant exchange that had left her nerves tight.

When he was out of sight she went into the house and crossed the day off on the calendar. It was still morning, much too early to cross it off but the ritual quieted her.

She turned the pages. Three more nights, two more full days to go. She would get through them somehow and not let him goad her into showing her feelings again. It gave him too much satisfaction.

Chapter 9

Mrs. Lane was the first one up the next morning. Usually the old man, who said he didn't need much sleep nowadays, was up ahead of her but that morning she was awake a little after six and knew immediately that she wouldn't be able to go back to sleep again. She tried, closing her eyes determinedly, but it did no good. There was too much awareness in her that tomorrow was the Fourth of July and that in two more days she would be free of Dan Ferris.

She might as well get up and work in the yard before the heat of the day set in.

She slid out of bed, went over to the window and looked out at the bright morning. She yawned as she stood there feeling sluggish and unrested. No wonder. She had lain awake until all hours, restless, uneasy, wishing it were Saturday and the old man was gone.

First thing in the morning, last thing at night, she thought wryly. Twenty-fours hours a day he was on her mind.

She got into shorts, blouse and sneakers, and tiptoed downstairs. She made herself a cup of instant coffee and went outdoors, startling into flight a flock of starlings spread out in a dark wave over the lawn.

The air was fresh, almost too cool for her light clothing, but she accomplished little in the yard. Her head felt heavy. She couldn't stop yawning. It was, she supposed, the result of months of accumulated tension which mounted higher and higher as release from it drew near.

At seven-thirty she put the garden tools away and went into the house to get breakfast. The old man was up. She heard him moving around overhead.

He came downstairs while she was setting the table. He was in a heavy mood himself and had little to say.

She read the paper during breakfast, not looking at him, not noticing how intently he kept looking at her, not really listening when he said, "Did you notice the date, Etta? It's July third."

She couldn't eat much. She still felt sluggish, her head still heavy.

A shower might help, she thought, while she was doing the dishes, but first she'd go down cellar and put a load in the washer.

Dan Ferris was settled in the living room with the paper when she went upstairs. His gaze followed her out of sight.

He gave her time to shower and get dressed before he went upstairs himself. He spent a few minutes in his room and then knocked on her door.

She had finished dressing and made her bed. She opened the door.

"Well, what is it?" she said.

"I want to show you something. It's in my room. Come and look."

His manner, half-excited, half-accusing puzzled her. "Show me what?" she asked.

"Something I had in my trunk. A reminder of the old days."

"Oh." She hesitated. "I don't know that I want to see it."

"It'll only take a minute. Come and look."

"Well, all right."

She followed him across the hall, halted abruptly in the doorway. "Oh now," she cried. "Oh, how could you?"

Sarah was in a virtuous mood when the Princes' phone rang a little later that morning. So far today she hadn't had a temper tantrum, hadn't jumped up and down on the floor even once when she discovered that Bobby had torn up a picture she'd drawn yesterday, the best picture she'd ever drawn in her life. Bobby had denied it at first which made her self-control all the more remarkable.

Now he was sulking in his room, permission to go swimming withdrawn as punishment for what he had done to tease Sarah and for lying about it afterward.

She couldn't resist peering in at him until he slammed the door in her face. Then she went out to her mother in the kitchen and said, "I bet I'll get another gold star today."

"I hope so," said Virginia.

School had closed two weeks ago. Soon thereafter, Sarah, beset with the frustrations of being the youngest, alternately snubbed and teased by Amy and Bobby whose advantage in age gave them many more privileges than she, had begun to have temper tantrums every day. This week her mother had tacked a sheet of paper with her name on it to their bulletin board and told her she would get a gold star beside her name for every day that she didn't have a tantrum. When she had seven of them there would be a special treat or prize for her.

So far Sarah had two and had high hopes of earning another today.

She was standing in front of the bulletin board admiring the two gold stars when the phone rang.

Her mother answered it.

It was Dan Ferris. "Good morning, Mrs. Prince," he said.

"Good morning, Mr. Ferris."

Sarah turned and drifted over to her mother when she heard the old man's name. She hadn't yet reconciled herself to his imminent departure.

"I've got a small project in mind this morning," he said. "It's Mrs. Lane's birthday next week and although I'll be gone by that time I'd like to get her something before I go and I'm wondering if Sarah would take a walk downtown with me and help pick it out."

"She's right here. I'll ask." Virginia turned to her daughter and relayed the message.

"Yes, yes." Sarah danced with joy. "Right now?"

"She's delighted," her mother informed the old man. "What time?"

"Well, as soon as she can come," he replied. "I thought we'd make it a special occasion, a farewell present for Sarah as well as my daughter-in-law, and then lunch at the inn."

"Why, how nice," said Virginia. "A real outing for her."

"I hope so," he said. "Gets me out from under my daughter-in-law's feet too. She has a terrible headache. I just told her to lie down and not worry about lunch for me or anything. So you tell Sarah to come along and we'll be off and let Etta have the house nice and quiet to herself."

"She'll be right over as soon as I get her into a dress for lunch at the inn. Will you try to have her back by two o'clock though? She'll need a nap."

Sarah shook her head vehemently as her mother hung up. "I won't need a nap," she said. "I want to stay all day."

Her mother didn't argue with her. She got her out of her shorts and into a sleeveless cotton dress, brushed her hair, supervised the washing of face and hands and in' five minutes had her on her way.

The old man met her at the back door as she came bounding up the steps. "Not so loud," he cautioned her putting his finger to his lips. "Mrs. Lane's lying down in the living room and for all we know she may be asleep."

He was ready to leave. He locked the back door and took Sarah's hand. "We'll go out the front door and lock it after us so no one can disturb her while we're gone," he said.

"Can I say good-by from the hall if she's still awake?" the little girl asked in a loud stage whisper.

He smiled. "Indeed you can, princess."

She tiptoed exaggeratedly beside him up the hall pausing in the living-room doorway. The shades were drawn to the window sills. Sarah pushed up her glasses and looked into the darkened room at Mrs. Lane lying on the sofa, slightly turned toward them, with a wet washcloth on her forehead and a bowl of ice water on the table in front of her. Her eyes were open although the washcloth almost covered them.

"See, she's awake," the child announced in the same

91

loud stage whisper.

"Yes, I'm awake, Sarah." Mrs. Lane's voice was muted, a little fretful. "I've got a dreadful headache, though, and I just want to be quiet. Run along now and have a nice time with Mr. Ferris."

"Yes, Mrs. Lane." Sarah pulled the old man toward the front door eager for their outing to begin. Then, remembering her manners, she turned back and said, "Good-by, Mrs. Lane. I hope you'll be all better soon."

"Thank you, Sarah. I hope so too."

They went out of the dimness into bright sunshine on the porch. Sarah skipped down the steps but the old man, about to close the front door, turned back at the sound of Mrs. Lane's voice calling, "Dan, will you just freshen this cloth again for me before you go?"

"Yes, Etta," he said and then over his shoulder to Sarah, "Wait out here, princess. I'll only be a minute."

He went back into the house. The little girl sat down on the bottom step, picked up a twig and began to prod a caterpillar with it.

The door was ajar but she did not listen to the conversation inside. Mrs. Lane sounded cross, she thought. But then, her mother sounded cross, too, when she was sick.

Everybody sounded cross when they got sick.

She studied the caterpillar crawling across the step. With fastidious care she eased it onto the twig and held it up in the air. Caterpillars, she thought, examining its underside, had a million funny little feet. What if their mothers had to buy shoes for every single one of them?

She was giggling at this thought when the old man

92

came out the door and beckoned her back up the steps. "Say good-by to Mrs. Lane again," he said in an undertone. "She feels so awful."

"Good-by, Mrs. Lane," Sarah called obediently through the screen door.

"Good-by honey."

"Take it easy now, Etta," the old man said.

"I will. The washcloth feels nice and cold." Mrs. Lane's voice sounded less fretful. "Enjoy yourselves."

"We will," they replied.

The old man shut the door and said, "Well, princess, we're off."

On the way downtown they discussed Mrs. Lane's birthday present.

"My mommy goes to Carroll's," the little girl informed him. "She says their things are nicer than Doane's."

"Then we'll go to Carroll's," the old man said.

Trees along the street formed a thick canopy overhead but even in their shade the day was hot.

"Only eleven o'clock too," the old man remarked looking at his watch. "Going to be a scorcher." He took out his handkerchief and wiped his face. "Let's have a Coke before we start shopping."

"I love Cokes," said Sarah.

They dawdled over them in the air-conditioned coolness of a drugstore. Carroll's just across the green, was air-conditioned too.

The saleswoman who came forward to serve them smiled at the contrast they made, the tall, white-haired old man and the small fair girl skipping along on short chubby legs to keep step with him.

Sarah wanted to look at everything, underwear,

blouses, dresses, costume jewelry, but in the end the old man bought a pocketbook of fine soft black leather for Mrs. Lane.

Sarah's eyes widened at the price, $24.95. "My Easter pocketbook only cost one dollar," she announced, adding on a falling note, "but it came from the five and ten."

"Well, that's all right for little girls," the saleswoman said.

She gift-wrapped the pocketbook. The old man waited until Sarah wandered away and then brought up the question of a pocketbook for her.

"Would that children's shop up the street have nice ones?" he asked.

"Yes, I'm sure they would. But her mother had the right idea, you know, buying one in the five and ten. She's too young for a good one."

"Still, if she'd like it," Dan Ferris said.

"A gift shouldn't be practical, you mean?" The saleswoman was charmed. She would tell the rest of the staff later what a sweet old fellow he was.

But when they reached the children's shop Sarah wasn't interested in a pocketbook. She picked out a fluffy toy dog, agonizing over making a choice between it and a pink rabbit.

It took time. It was after one o'clock before they settled down in the inn dining room for lunch and nearly two when they finished, the old man bearing in mind Mrs. Prince's mention of Sarah's nap.

The heat was smothering when they emerged from the coolness of the inn. They walked slowly, the old man carrying Mrs. Lane's gift, Sarah carrying her own, her face flushed, her hair clinging to it in damp wisps. But she was content. She would have her toy dog to show and much to tell when she got home.

As they approached Mrs. Lane's she asked, "Are you going to give her her present right away?"

"Well, I have to give it to her ahead of time but I haven't thought about when."

"Why don't you give it to her now?"

"I might at that." He paused. "Would you like to be there when I do, princess, or give it to her yourself?"

"Oh yes."

Sarah looked excited but then the old man's face turned doubtful. "You're supposed to get home for your nap," he reminded her.

"It'll only take a few minutes and I'm not a bit sleepy."

"Well, I'll tell you what." They were in front of the house as he offered his compromise. "We'll go in quietly and if Mrs. Lane is asleep we won't wake her up. I'll put her present aside and you go have your nap and come back and give it to her later."

The little girl's face fell. Later was forever away.

"Maybe she'll be awake," she said hopefully.

They went up the walk to the front porch. The door was still closed and locked as they had left it. The old man took out his key and admitted them. They went into the house quietly, Sarah slipping past him and stopping short in the living-room doorway.

"She's not here," she said.

He looked into the room. The shades were still drawn, the washcloth lay in the bowl on the table, the pillow still showed the hollow where her head had rested but there was no sign of her.

"She must have gone up to her room," he said.

"Or maybe she's outdoors," Sarah suggested. "Shall I go look?"

"Yes, and see if her car's in the garage. I'll look upstairs."

Sarah went out the front door and he went upstairs.

Mrs. Lane wasn't in her room or anywhere else on the second floor. He opened the attic door and called her name but there was no answer.

Sarah climbed the stairs announcing that Mrs. Lane wasn't in the yard but that her car was in the garage. "Maybe she got better and went somewheres with somebody," she added.

"That's possible. Let's go see if she left a note."

They went downstairs. There was no note on Mrs. Lane's desk.

"I'll look on the kitchen table," said Sarah darting out through the dining room. The next moment she said, "No note but the cellar door's open, Mr. Ferris. Maybe she's down there."

The cellar stairs ran under the stairway to the second floor. The door was at the rear end of the hall. The little girl headed toward it from the kitchen calling, "Mrs. Lane, Mrs. Lane, are you down cellar?"

She gave a strangled gasp as the old man went out into the hall from the living room. Then she screamed and went on screaming at the top of her lungs.

She was pressed back against the open door when he reached her. Mrs. Lane lay sprawled out at the foot of the cellar stairs, her jaw slack, her eyes rolled up in her head. Anyone, even a child as young as Sarah, would know she was dead just to look at her but Dan Ferris ran down the stairs, lifted her body as if something could be done for her and then, after a moment laid it down again, straightening it out, smoothing down her skirt.

Sarah still stood against the door, glasses hanging off her nose, emitting her ear-piercing screams as unremittingly as a siren.

The old man's heart pounded. He climbed the stairs slowly, clutching the railing, muttering to the child with no prospect of making himself heard, "I guess she fell so fast she had no chance to catch hold of it."

He coaxed Sarah away from the cellar door and closed it. She was more rigid than the dead woman in whose body rigor mortis hadn't yet set in.

His knees trembled as he led the little girl into the living room. He sat down and drew her down on his lap. He made soothing sounds and rocked her gently until her screams dwindled into hiccuping sobs.

She was manageable now, he thought.

"Sarah," he said.

She held tight to him and burrowed deeper into his shoulder. He plucked off her glasses and laid them on the arm of the chair.

"Sarah, I'm going to leave you here in this chair while I call your mother to come over. You want her, don't you?"

"Y-yes."

"Then let go of me so I can call her."

She let go. He deposited her in the chair, a bundle of misery, went to the telephone and called Mrs. Prince.

After her first horrified exclamations she wasted no time on questions. "I'll be right over," she said.

He went back to Sarah. The police would have to be

called but that could wait until the child's mother arrived. He was an old man. He was entitled to a few minutes to compose himself before he did anything.

He needed that interval. He had wished Etta ill, yes, he had to look at what had happened to her as no more than her due, but he also had to think of himself, how it would effect him in the immediate present and the future.

He had Sarah on his lap again but hardly noticed her in his absorption with self.

She looked at him uncertainly and drew away a little. He looked different. His face had changed in a way that made her feel very uncomfortable.

She wished her mother would hurry up and get there.

Chapter 10

"She was more sprawled out," Dan Ferris said on a hesitant note. "Maybe a little to one side. I could see her face, though, from the top of the stairs."

The medical examiner, kneeling on the cellar floor beside Mrs. Lane's body, exploring broken bone and matted tissue behind the right ear, said nothing. The police chief, on the scene himself with other officers, exchanged glances with the sergeant. They preferred bodies undisturbed until they arrived to examine them.

A small amount of dried blood had already been found on the cellar floor.

The medical examiner stood up dusting off the knees of his trousers.

"She probably fell the full flight and landed on her head," he said. "No other visible injuries except a contusion on the knee. But still, alone here and all, nothing to lose by an autopsy. Dr. Martin will do it."

"Our emergency wagon will be along in a few minutes," the chief said. "How long would you say she's been dead, Doctor?"

"Well, you know how rigor mortis varies, but it's

setting in. She's been dead four to five hours maybe."

The police chief looked at his watch. "Three-ten now. Mr. Ferris says he left before eleven. She must have died soon after that."

"Probably as close as we'll come," the medical examiner said. He left then saying that he would be in touch later. The police chief, whose name was Healey, suggested to Dan Ferris that they go upstairs.

The old man followed him. They sat down in the living room where nothing had been touched except the window shades which had been rolled up.

Two officers were still examining the cellar. Otherwise, they were alone in the house. Virginia Prince had taken Sarah home as soon as the police arrived, Healey telling her they would question the child later.

"Let's just go over the whole thing again, Mr. Ferris," he said when they were seated.

But before they could begin the emergency wagon appeared and Mrs. Lane's body was carried out on a stretcher. A small crowd had collected across the street and watched solemnly.

Dan Ferris shed tears while this was going on. Wiping his eyes he excused himself. "She was so good to me," he said. "She was all I had."

Healey's rough-hewn face softened as he looked at the bowed white head. He signaled the sergeant who was in the hall to come in and take notes.

The old man straightened up and put away his

handkerchief. "So good to me," he repeated.

He was stalling for time. He couldn't make up his mind whether or not to mention the money he'd got out of Etta Lane. He didn't know how thorough the investigation would be. If the money was bound to come to police attention it would look better for him to bring it up himself here and now than to have them bring it up later. On the other hand, if they didn't go into her financial situation, they might never find out about it at all.

Let it alone, he decided. An accidental death wasn't like a murder.

"Would you like a glass of water?" Healey inquired.

The old man shook his head. He stared at the bowl on the table with the washcloth in it. "I put ice in it," he said. "I wrung the cloth out and put it on her forehead. She said it made her head feel better. She called me back to freshen it as the little girl and I were leaving."

"She complained of a headache this morning, you said, but got breakfast, did the dishes and so on?"

"Yes. And then took a shower and got dressed. But her headache got worse."

"Did she take anything for it?"

"I don't know. She said she'd lie down. I went upstairs and got a pillow from her bed and the washcloth —"

Dan Ferris's voice faltered. "I fixed the ice water and drew the shades —"

He was silent for so long that the police chief prompted him. "Then you and the little girl went downtown?"

"Yes." He described their outing, the shopping they'd done, lunch at the inn, their return home.

"The worst of it was"—he paused to collect himself—"for little Sarah to find her. We looked all over the house and then she was the one who spotted the cellar door open."

"I wonder why she went down cellar when she didn't feel well," Healey said.

The sergeant intervened. "The washer and dryer are down there, sir. Clem looked and said there's a load of wet clothes in the washer."

"Oh, that's right, I heard her go down after breakfast," Dan Ferris said.

The police chief nodded. Mrs. Lane had remembered the wash and started down cellar to put it in the dryer.

The reason for her fall was more obscure. There was no obstruction, nothing she could have tripped over on the stairs. She was wearing low-heeled shoes, straight skirt and tailored blouse that couldn't have caught on anything. Her headache might have brought on a dizzy spell or she might have taken some sedative that confused her.

The old man shook his head when these possibilities were mentioned to him. "I don't know," he said. "It was the first headache she'd had since I came."

Healey fell silent reviewing the case as it had

developed so far. The call from Mrs. Prince had been logged at 2:25, the nearest cruiser had been on the scene within five minutes and he himself, Clem Oliver, and Sergeant Carlson within another ten. The old man said he'd found the house just as he left it, front and back doors locked. There were no signs of forced entry or of anyone admitted by Mrs. Lane. She had apparently been alone until her fatal fall which had occurred not long after Ferris and the little girl left.

It all seemed perfectly straightforward. Ferris seemed perfectly straightforward himself, shocked by Mrs. Lane's death and in no way to blame for it. According to him, they were very fond of each other and the fact that he had been visiting her since March bore him out.

There were always ifs, of course. If the autopsy showed anything questionable, or if the little girl's story differed from Ferris's or if it turned out he and Mrs. Lane weren't as devoted as he said or if he stood to gain by her death they might want to take a closer look at the accident that brought it about.

In that case, had some kind of a booby trap been set for her?

The classic one was a string or cord invisible to the naked eye fastened across a step to trip over.

Maybe he'd better have Clem examine the door-jambs for nail or screw marks. It would have to be the doorjambs if anywhere. The cellar handrail had no uprights to fasten anything to.

103

How could Ferris be sure she'd go down cellar though?

He knew there was a load in the washer. She might have mentioned that she had to put it in the dryer.

The doorjambs had better be looked at right away.

Healey excused himself, went to the head of the cellar stairs and summoned Clem Oliver, telling him in an undertone what he wanted. There was a magnifying glass in the lab kit. His subordinate nodded and went back down cellar to get it.

The police chief returned to the living room and asked about Mrs. Lane's next of kin.

The past with which he had blackmailed Etta Lane suddenly loomed large and threatening in the old man's mind. He didn't care on his own account if it came out now — he was perfectly blameless — but it might raise a question about the money he'd got from Etta.

He made haste to explain that he was the nearest thing to next of kin that the dead woman had. "She was an only child," he said. "Her father and mother died years ago and there were just a few distant cousins she'd lost all track of. She mentioned it to me several times, that she was glad I came because she felt so alone in the world."

Her will might tell them something about her family, Healey reflected, but if the old man had the facts straight there'd be no mention of relatives. It would be up to her executor to take charge of her burial and straighten out her affairs.

Dan Ferris had a question of his own. "Was it because I moved her that there'll have to be an autopsy?" he inquired. "I don't like the thought of it—her poor body all cut up."

"It was the medical examiner's decision. He might have had more in mind than determining the extent and nature of her injuries. If she took something for her headache that made her dizzy or confused it would explain her fall. It's too bad you moved her, of course."

"I know," the old man said meekly. "But at a time like that your mind leaves you, the shock and all. I just ran down the stairs and picked her up as if there was something I could do for her. Then when I put her down I couldn't help straightening her out to make her look decent."

"Still, in a case like this, it's better not to touch the body at all."

His statement sounded ridiculous to him even as he made it. How many dead bodies was the old man likely to find in the future? How many dead bodies did the average person come across in a lifetime?

Oliver appeared in the doorway. "Could I speak to you, sir?"

Healey followed him to the far end of the hall out of earshot of Dan Ferris.

"Negative, sir, on the doorjambs," said Oliver. "No marks of any kind."

"Well, it was just a thought." Healey went back

to the living room. There was nothing more for him to do here. The inquiry into Mrs. Lane's death would fan out in other directions including a talk with her lawyer concerning her will.

Soon after Healey's departure the other officers left, the sergeant asking the old man if he'd like to have one of neighbors come in or if there was anything he could do for him.

"I'll be all right," Dan Ferris replied. "I'd just as soon be alone for a little while and pull myself together."

The police had hardly left, however, before the phone rang. It was Virginia Prince asking if he'd like to come to their house or if he'd rather she came to him.

He gave her the same answer he'd given the sergeant, adding, "But it's very kind of you to think of me, Mrs. Prince."

"Not at all," she said. "But you must come to dinner tonight. We have it around six."

He accepted the invitation. "I'll lie down for a while first," he said. "I need to rest."

"Of course you do," she replied sympathetically.

He remembered to ask how Sarah was.

"Well, a little subdued, but over the worst of the shock."

"Good," he said. "She left the toy dog I bought her. It's here on the table with Etta's" — a catch came into his voice — "birthday present. I'll bring it along." He cleared his throat. "I'm sorry Sarah had to be involved in this. I never dreamed when we went off on our outing—"

"How could you? Don't give it another thought."

The old man did not lie down when he hung up. He had answered the phone in the kitchen and went straight to the liquor cabinet. What he needed was a good stiff drink.

He made himself one and stood at the kitchen window drinking it, thinking about Etta Lane's lawyer, wondering if he knew how much money she had, worrying, fretting over it.

But not over the dead woman herself, not really. Her death had a rightness to it balanced against Jimmy's.

Chapter 11

Sergeant Carlson questioned Sarah the next morning.

It was the Fourth of July. Ray Prince was home and both parents were present during the questioning. Sarah was brought in from the yard by her mother while Amy and Bobby were told to stay outdoors. They settled down under the open living-room windows to hear all they could of what went on inside. Sarah had gained status in their eyes. They were impressed by her role in a police investigation.

She was impressed herself. She bustled into the living room self-importantly and then was suddenly overcome with shyness at the sight of the officer in uniform.

He smiled and said hello and soon set her at ease, telling her he had a little girl who was three and asking how old she was.

Three was mere babyhood. Sarah couldn't help feeling superior. "I'm going to be five next week," she said.

"Next month," her mother inserted.

"Well, next month." She blew her hair out of her

eyes and pushed up her glasses for an open inspection of the sergeant. "How soon will your little girl be four?" she asked.

"Not until November."

"Oh. What's her name?"

"Brenda."

"Is it?" she gave him a pleased grin. "I have a friend named Brenda. She lives down the street."

"Well, isn't that a coincidence," he said.

It made them friends practically. After a few more preliminaries the sergeant brought up Mrs. Lane.

Sarah's face sobered. She buried her head in her mother's lap. "She got killed dead," she said. "She fell down the cellar stairs. The door was open and I looked—"

"Yes, I know." Sergeant Carlson waited a moment and then said, "Let's go back before that. Let's start with when you first went to the house yesterday morning."

The child lifted her tousled head. "Mrs. Lane had a headache. It hurted her bad, I guess. She was lying on the sofa. Mr. Ferris said maybe she was asleep but she wasn't. She was awake. She had a washcloth over her face."

"Her face?"

"Do you mean forehead, Sarah?" Virginia interjected.

The little girl nodded. "Yes, her forehead. There was a bowl with ice cubes on the table."

"Did Mrs. Lane talk to you?" the sergeant inquired.

The little girl nodded again.

"What did she say?"

Sarah gave him a faraway look and was silent, chin propped in her hands, elbows resting on the arm of her mother's chair.

"Well, Sarah?" her father prodded from across the room.

Her gaze drifted to him. "I don't remember," she said at last. "It wasn't nothing much."

"Anything much," her mother corrected her.

Back went the blue, blue eyes to the sergeant. "It wasn't anything much," she said solemnly. "Wanna see me do a headstand?"

"Sarah!" Her mother took her by the arm. "Sergeant Carlson asked you a question. Answer it please."

"I don't remember," said Sarah, "but I guess she said hello or something. And I guess she hoped we'd have a nice time."

"And then?"

"We left." Sarah slid out of her mother's grasp and sat down on the floor. "Oh, we said good-by." She glanced up at her mother. "And I remembered my manners like you're always telling me. I said I hoped she'd feel better."

"That was nice," said Virginia.

"Yes, it was." The little girl turned a somersault ending upright beside her father, was told to behave herself and turned another somersault that brought her back to her mother.

"We didn't leave yet though," she informed the sergeant. "When we were on the porch and Mr. Ferris was going to close the door Mrs. Lane called him back to fix the cloth on her face—her forehead. She wanted him to put it in the ice water again."

Sarah paused in thought. "I guess it helped her head not to hurt." She leaned against her mother's chair. "Like when I had a temperature last spring, Mommy."

"Last winter."

"Well, all right, last winter."

"Did you go back in the house with Mr. Ferris?" Carlson asked.

"No. He said to wait on the porch, he'd just be a minute. So I sat down and waited."

"Did he come right back out?" Carlson's tone was casual but he had more than a casual interest in Sarah's answer. He and the police chief didn't really think the old man, going back into the house, had somehow got Mrs. Lane to the cellar door and pushed her down the stairs; they thought her fall was as accidental as it looked; but it was their job to consider every possibility.

The front door, whether it was open or closed, came under that heading. Ferris might have been able to lure Mrs. Lane to the cellar door without attracting Sarah's attention but she would have made some sort of outcry when the old man pushed her down the stairs. He wouldn't have risked it with the front door open.

111

"Did Mr. Ferris close the front door when he went back in the house?" the sergeant asked.

Sarah's parents shot startled glances at him but she was matter-of-fact in her reply.

"The door closes by itself," she said.

"The screen door yes. I mean the inside door." She gave it thought. "I guess it was open."

"Did you look?"

"No, but I could hear them talking inside."

"What did they say?"

The sergeant earned himself a severe look. "I didn't listen. My mommy says it's not polite to listen when people are talking in the other room."

"Sometimes we can't help hearing what they say."

"But I didn't listen."

"Then what happened?"

"Mr. Ferris came out. He said good-by to Mrs. Lane again and he said I should say good-by again too. So I did. And she said good-by to us."

"This was after Mr. Ferris came back out?"

"Yes. Like I just told you."

"Sarah," her mother admonished but she and her husband exchanged relieved glances.

That was that. Out the window went the tenuous possibility that Ferris had pushed Mrs. Lane down the cellar stairs while Sarah waited for him on the front porch.

There was another possibility, even more tenuous, that had to be explored: that Ferris had left Sarah downtown somewhere, returned to the house, accomplished the murder of Mrs. Lane and hurried back to the child.

But Sarah's detailed account of what they had done downtown erased that possibility immediately. Nowhere was there a time gap that would have allowed the old man to return to the house.

There was no need for further inquiries, Carlson reflected on his way back to the police station. The case could be closed as an accidental death as soon as they heard from the pathologist—unless there was something in his report to raise fresh doubt. Sergeant Carlson didn't think there would be. Particularly now, in view of Mrs. Lane's will which Healey had tracked down yesterday. Her estate, her lawyer estimated, would run between one hundred and twenty-five and one hundred and fifty thousand but no individual would profit from it. It all went to charity. They had half-expected a recent codicil leaving some sort of bequest to Ferris but there wasn't one. Perhaps she hadn't got around to it.

The sergeant made his report to Healey when he got back to the police station.

"Well, that's the end of it," the chief said. "I just had a call from Dr. Martin. The head injury was the sole cause of death. Occipital fracture, brain damage and so forth. She'd taken no drugs, not even an aspirin so we have to assume a dizzy spell from her headache caused her fall." Healey paused. "Martin did say he would have expected more contusions and lacerations from it, but there was only one, the bruise on the knee."

113

"Well, funny things can happen in a fall," the sergeant commented. "Like car accidents where sometimes the impact isn't too great and yet someone gets killed; and another time the car will be reduced to scrap but the driver will walk away from it with hardly a scratch."

Healey nodded agreement. They went over it all briefly for the last time. There were no loose ends still to be investigated. There were not even relatives to be notified. The bank, executor of the will, and the lawyer would have to make the funeral arrangements.

Before the police chief left to take up his interrupted holiday the case was marked closed.

Chapter 12

Mrs. Lane's funeral took place the day before John Frear returned from his business trip. His sister phoned him as soon as he was home and he went immediately, stunned and saddened, to pay a sympathy call on the old man.

He was surprised at the depth of his feeling. He hadn't known Etta Lane very long and yet he felt bereft; he felt that they had made a start toward a relationship that might have become important to both of them. He found it painful to ring the bell at her front door where he had said good-by to her only two weeks ago looking forward to the cookout she would have for him when he got back.

Dan Ferris welcomed him cordially, accepting his condolences with a bereaved air. They sat down in the living room, Frear declining the drink offered, already half sorry he had come and yet aware of his need to learn at firsthand the details of Etta Lane's death.

The old man supplied them with pauses for deep sighs.

"Seems so strange, a headache leading to her death," Frear said at the end with a sigh of his own. "One night playing bridge someone mentioned having one and she said she was lucky, she

115

never had them, couldn't remember when she'd last had one."

The old man shrugged. "Well, you know how women are, especially a widow like Etta, getting on toward fifty. She wouldn't want to say her health wasn't perfect, least of all to a single man like you."

The remark rubbed Frear the wrong way. One of the things he had liked about Etta Lane was her lack of small feminine evasions. He couldn't imagine her covering up a small thing like a headache.

"I doubt she'd bother to lie about it," he said crisply.

"Well . . . just an idea." Another shrug. "Poor Etta. Makes no difference now, one way or the other."

Frear didn't answer. He looked around the room. It was orderly enough—the old man was too neat to leave things around—but it already showed small signs of change. Bowls and vases that had always been filled with flowers when he'd been here before were empty now, there was a film of dust on the furniture, an air of neglect in the room; it was as if it knew it wouldn't have again the particular care and attention it was used to.

It was a depressing thought; a depressing room. He wished he hadn't come. He no longer found Dan Ferris a pleasant old fellow. His sighs and headshakes seemed put on, overdone. Frear found himself doubting suddenly that he had really been devoted to Etta Lane. Thinking back, he couldn't recall that she herself had ever said he was; he'd heard it from others, his sister, his brother-in-law.

There was nothing here for him. Learning the details of Etta's death, expressing sympathy that with his new feeling toward the old man seemed uncalled for, did not alter the fact that she was gone and that he would never see her again.

He would like to have a picture of her, even a snapshot, but he wouldn't ask for one. There was something about the way the old man looked at him, almost as if he read his thoughts and took some sort of satisfaction out of . . .

God, he'd better get out of here before he let his imagination run away with him completely.

He stood up. "I'll have to run along now, Mr. Ferris."

"So soon?" The old man's face changed taking on a lonely look.

Well, he probably was lonely here by himself but wouldn't he be leaving soon? He was supposed to have left last week. Now that Etta's funeral was over there was no reason for him to stay.

Dan Ferris walked to the door with him, looked out at the lawn and said, "Grass needs mowing. I've got to pull myself together and take care of things around here."

"Oh, I thought you'd be leaving. You were planning to, weren't you?"

"I was, but—" The old man gave him a secretive

look. "I might change my mind. I just might."

Frear didn't pursue the subject. He wasn't interested. All he wanted was to get away.

The old man went out on the porch with him and stood there until his car vanished from sight. Then he went back inside and halted in the living-room doorway looking around uncertainly.

Funny how empty the house seemed without Etta. He'd been alone in it any number of times since he'd been here but the emptiness hadn't felt the same. He'd known those times, of course, that she'd be back.

But this time she was never coming back. She was out there in the cemetery, Hillcrest, Hillside— what was the name of it? Didn't matter. She was out there and there she would stay until the end of time.

Funny, the lost sinking feeling it gave him.

He didn't have anything to think about, that was it. There was scarcely a day or night since Jimmy died that he hadn't thought about Etta, hated her, lain awake nights trying to figure out some way to track her down.

Now it was all over and it left him as empty as her house. Like losing a job you'd been going to for twenty-seven years and suddenly you were fired, the whole routine and purpose of your life stripped away, leaving you with nothing to do, nothing to get up for, no plans to make . . .

But of course there were. Plans for himself, his

future, years of it ahead of him probably. Good years with money in the bank, health to enjoy it, the weight of Etta off his back.

First, though, he had to get over this queer empty feeling. It would take a little time, that was all. No need to worry about it, no need to worry about anything. Just this morning the man from the bank had told him that.

Take your time making plans, Mr. Ferris, the man had said. No need to worry about the house, about anything right now. Just look after it, keep things up until we see where we are.

Take your time, Mr. Ferris. No rush, no need to worry about anything.

The man didn't have any idea how empty the house felt.

Not that it wasn't good riddance to Etta. It was justice that she'd died like that. Poetic justice. Biblical justice. An eye for an eye . . .

The old man straightened his sagging shoulders and went to the kitchen to make himself a drink. He'd be all right; he'd get over this feeling he had. Meanwhile, he'd keep busy. Mow the lawn tomorrow, tidy up the yard. Take a walk, maybe over to the Princes'. Little girl hadn't been around lately.

There was still Ella too. Although her existence had to be kept a secret.

He took a walk over to the Princes' the next afternoon but didn't see Sarah. She wasn't home. No one was home but Virginia who seated him on

119

the terrace and served iced tea.

That night after the children were in bed she said to her husband thoughtfully, "You know, from the way Mr. Ferris spoke today, he's going to be here a while. He's lost heart for any trip, he told me, and doesn't know what he wants to do. The man at the bank who's in charge of Mrs. Lane's estate told him there was no hurry about leaving. They'll put the house up for sale but meanwhile he can stay on rent free and look after it for them."

"Oh." Ray Prince wasn't particularly interested. "Let's see, what's on tonight?" He opened the newspaper to the TV section.

But Virginia caught his attention when she added, "He said a couple of things that made me wonder if he was thinking of buying the house himself."

"That's plain nuts. What would he want with a six- or seven-room house and a pretty big one too at his age?"

"Well, perhaps because of its associations with Mrs. Lane. After all, he's been pretty footloose since his son died, and perhaps these few months here with her have been the closest thing to family life he's had in years. It's sort of pathetic when you stop to think about it."

Ray Prince eyed his wife over the top of the newspaper. "Didn't you tell me when he first came that Sarah got the impression Mrs. Lane didn't want him there?"

"Yes, but that was just at the beginning and you know how Sarah exaggerates. She only mentioned it that once anyway. And look how she adores him."

Virginia paused, playing back in her mind what she had just said, then added, "Although she hasn't been near him since Mrs. Lane's death. Not that I would have let her intrude but she hasn't even asked to go. She's got some kind of a mixed-up feeling about it."

"What else would you expect after what happened?"

"It's not just that." Virginia wrinkled her forehead in thought. "Tonight going to bed, right out of the blue—we weren't talking about anything connected with it—Sarah said she didn't think Mr. Ferris was really sorry Mrs. Lane was dead."

"She say why?"

"Well, she said he had a funny look on his face while they were waiting for me to get there. He acted funny, she said. But she wouldn't—probably couldn't—explain what she meant by it. So I just dropped it."

"Only thing to do. The sooner she forgets the whole thing the better."

Ray Prince got to his feet to turn on the TV set. But before he touched the knobs he looked at his wife and said firmly, "Even if Sarah gets over this feeling she has, I don't want her going there any more. It was one thing for her to run in and out

121

of the house when Mrs. Lane was alive but it's an entirely different proposition now that Ferris is living there alone."

Virginia raised her eyebrows. "Ray, you surely don't mean—?"

"I mean just what I said. Sarah is not to set foot in that house again unless you or I or some other responsible person is with her."

"But he's such a nice old man—"

"Sure he is—far as we know. But if he stays on there by himself he might start getting some peculiar ideas. It's been known to happen. Old men living alone aren't what I'd call suitable companions for little girls."

Virginia was silent considering what he had said. He was right, of course. She hadn't thought of it that way herself, but he was right. Sarah's friendship with the old man that had meant so much to her these past months was over. Her father had ruled against it.

But wasn't it over, anyway, the day Mrs. Lane died? From the way Sarah acted, it seemed so.

For her that day the magic grandfather had lost his magic.

He bought the house in September. The bank had appraised it at sixteen thousand but let him have it for fifteen, taking into account possible delay in selling it elsewhere and the realtor's commission that would have to be paid.

For several hundred dollars more the furnishing

were included in the sale.

The old man felt good walking home from the bank the day he took title to the property. He did sums in his head. He had nine thousand left out of what he'd got from Etta; he'd leave one-third of it in the bank as an emergency fund and invest the rest in good solid stocks such as she herself had owned. Not that he knew much about them, but he'd been studying the financial section of the paper lately and there were plenty of them that would keep his money safe and make it grow.

He wouldn't invest through that fellow Etta had dealt with though. He would give him a wide berth.

With dividends and bank interest, his social security and his own small savings he'd get along fine; he'd be a man of affairs living as snug as a bug in a rug in his comfortable house.

These pleasurable musings occupied most of the walk home but near the end of it his thoughts turned to Etta. Going up the front walk he caught himself thinking that she would be waiting for him inside.

It was funny the way he kept thinking that. There was another thing too; Etta and Ella tended to merge in his thoughts lately. It was becoming a habit with him. He'd better watch it.

1925

Chapter 13

Deep in the shadows of the alley he stood watching the stage door. Young had emerged from it minutes ago, walked out to the street and headed south. No need to follow him. He would stick to the same procedure that had worked successfully—or so they both thought—earlier this week and last week in Rushville. Young would wait for the trolley two stations on, Etta would board it one stop before him. They would sit apart acting like strangers during the ride to Young's apartment. He would get off at the nearest corner to it, she would ride another block, get off and walk back. It would be close to midnight when they arrived. There'd be no one on the street and the apartment house would be pretty much in darkness except for lights in the halls.

It was a small rundown place in a backwater neighborhood catering to transients but too far from the Lyric to draw theater people. It was, in short, an ideal place for a faithless woman to meet her paramour.

The June night was unseasonably chilly. He buttoned his coat and turned up the collar against a mean little wind that whipped through the alley scattering bits of debris before it.

He tensed as the stage door opened but it wasn't Etta. It was Flo and her partner in her mind-reading act, chatting and laughing as they moved up the alley to the street.

His gaze followed her broad figure scornfully. She was the one Etta had told Jimmy she was visiting after the show tonight; Flo was her cover, condoning her adultery. It was like seeking like. Flo herself had no more morals than an alley cat.

The pair vanished from sight. They were the last to leave except Etta.

The stage door opened and she appeared, looking this way and that before she hurried out to the street.

Dan Ferris drifted after her. She turned south at the entrance to the alley, he turned north to the trolley stop around the corner.

He was just in time for the trolley. Etta would have to hurry to catch it two stops on.

There was only a handful of passengers at this time of night. He made his way, as he had the last time, to the rear seat, slid down low on it and pulled his coat collar higher, his hat down over his face, giving the impression of a man asleep on his way home.

Etta boarded the trolley a block beyond the theater, shot a quick glance around her and seated herself in the middle of the car, her face turned to the window. She did not look at Young when he climbed aboard at the next stop and with his eyes straight ahead a few seats away from her.

The trolley run to his apartment was about a mile. The rest was a repeat of the other night, Young getting off at his corner, Etta a block on, Dan Ferris at the next stop.

She was just a small, slim silhouette ahead of him, head bent as if fearful of recognition even on this poorly lighted side street.

She should hang her head, Dan Ferris thought grimly. She should never hold it up again as long as she lived.

Trim and fit in his middle forties he had to slacken his stride so as not to close the distance between them, making no sound in his rubber-soled shoes, keeping in the shadow of the buildings.

When Etta reached the apartment house Young stepped out of the doorway. Their figures joined in a brief embrace and broke apart as they turned toward the door and were lost to sight inside.

Dan Ferris drew abreast of the building and halted at the edge of the sidewalk looking up at the second floor front. A light went on there, stayed on for a few minutes and went out.

Young had mentioned his apartment backstage, a bedsitting room, kitchenette and bath. He had rented it for the week he played the Lyric. Dan Ferris could picture all too well what was going on up there, the light turned on to find their way in, then turned out as they settled down to their love-

129

making.

The street light shone on the peeling paint of the yellow brick front with the sign that read: FURNISHED APTS. BY WEEK OR MONTH, INQUIRE APT. 1-A WITHIN. It shone on the ragged foundation plantings, the strip of thin grass that separated the building from the sidewalk.

It wasn't much different from the apartment house Dan Ferris had trailed them to last week in Rushville.

Love Nests. The phrase leaped into his mind. Cheap, fly-by-night love nests for rent by the week or month. Inquire Apt. 1-A within.

Etta, his fastidious, touch-me-not daughter-in-law, lying to Jimmy, sneaking off to a dump like this with Young, the big, muscular, handsome acrobat, strutting backstage for her benefit, watching his moment to catch her eye.

They'd all been playing the same circuit most of the time for the past three months. Etta had been seeing more and more of Young right under Jimmy's nose. Poor, blind trusting Jimmy . . .

If he didn't have his father to look out for him where would he be?

Dan Ferris walked away toward the street where the trolley line ran. There was nothing to stay for. The routine followed at these illicit meetings would be repeated. Etta would stay with the fellow for an hour or more, then he'd come out of the building with her, put her in the taxi he'd called and say good night. Etta would ride back to their rooming house and not make a sound slipping into the room she shared with Jimmy across the hall from Dan Ferris. Tomorrow she'd look at them out of those big blue eyes of hers and fuss over what Jimmy ate for breakfast like a good little wife, like the little innocent she was supposed to be when Jimmy brought her into their lives three years ago.

The slut, the two-timing slut, he raged, walking past the first trolley stop he came to, walking fast, trying to ease the burning, consuming rage within him.

How dared she do this to Jimmy or, for that matter, himself? Hadn't he been all kindness to her from the day Jimmy brought her, his bride, to meet him, her new father-in-law, who'd had no warning or preparation for Jimmy's running off and getting married like that? Hadn't he welcomed her as a daughter without a word of reproach and worked up a new act to include her? Hadn't he taught her what little she knew about how to carry herself on stage and speak her few lines—all she was capable of, not having an ounce of acting ability in her whole body—so that she could be heard in the back of the house?

Hadn't he done everything, in fact, that a man could do for a little nobody from nowhere Jimmy had picked up, falling for big blue eyes and shining blonde hair and a smile like an angel?

And what thanks had he got for all he'd done? Cool politeness and nagging at Jimmy to get out of show business, make a home for her with never a thought for her father-in-law, not getting any younger, hanging on to the only life he knew.

The two-timing slut. Giving herself to that oaf back there, betraying Jimmy, betraying him. . . .

Dan Ferris saw the lights of the trolley approaching from behind him and quickened his step to the next stop.

It was close to midnight. He was the only passenger. The motorman was ready to chat when he paid his fare but he brushed past him and took a rear seat.

He stared out the window on the ride back, his face set in smouldering fury. Etta thought she was getting away with it but this was her last night with Young. Tomorrow night after the show — no use upsetting him before they went on — he'd tell Jimmy the whole story. No, not tomorrow night when they were taking the midnight bus to Grayport where they opened at the Rialto over the Fourth of July. Young was playing there too. He'd be on the bus. Dan Ferris would have to wait to tell Jimmy about his wife until he could get him alone in Grayport.

He lay awake most of the night. He heard Etta come in an hour after him, tiptoe upstairs, open and close her bedroom door quietly. She would, no doubt, undress in the dark so as not to awaken Jimmy.

Poor Jimmy. A decenter, cleaner-living fellow was never brought up in show business. He'd always been a loyal, obedient son, a credit to his parents. Molly had raised him for it on her death-bed. After she was gone they'd carried on together, everything fine until Jimmy fell head over heels in love with Etta and married her overnight. Then the old closeness, the unquestioning loyalty he'd had from Jimmy became a thing of the past. She'd made him restless, uncertain of what the future offered in vaudeville. So far he hadn't really tried to break away but she kept after him like water wearing away stone.

It was a good guess that she'd have won out sooner or later; but not now, not when he told Jimmy what kind of a wife she was. Then she'd be out of their lives as fast as she had come into them.

Dan Ferris turned over in his bed and looked out the window at the night sky.

That was what he wanted, wasn't it? Etta gone, everything the way it used to be?

They'd have to work up a new act, go back, maybe, to the one they'd had before Etta and Ella.

It didn't matter. They were playing the last booking of their contract in Grayport. Then he'd grab a train to Chicago and talk to Sam about future bookings for the two Ferrises — or should it be three? No, they couldn't build their act around Ella; there'd be no place for her without Etta.

Sam wouldn't be too pleased. He thought the four Ferrises was the best act they'd had in years. He'd have to accept it, though, find what bookings he could for them. That was what an agent

133

was for.

It would all work out somehow. Jimmy would feel bad at first but he'd get over it and in the end thank his father for finding out the truth about Etta. Then they'd be closer than ever before.

Jimmy wouldn't be so quick to trust another woman either. He'd been too trusting of Etta all along, that was the trouble. A man should keep his wife under his thumb. He'd always done that with Molly and kept her faithful to him, guided by what he wanted, all her days.

Jimmy, unfortunately, lacked his father's strength of character, didn't take after him in that respect. Now, if he himself were married to Etta . . .

He quelled that thought on the instant. It wasn't new; it had a way of slipping in . . .

She'd soon be gone though. He wouldn't have to worry about any thoughts he had of her once Jimmy heard what she'd been up to.

She'd be gone. He would not see her again, big blue eyes, satiny complexion, beautiful hair. He would not see again that angelic smile, that sunny smile, sunny, that was, for everyone but him.

Right from the first she'd shown reserve that he couldn't break down toward him.

God, how he hated her!

Yes, he hated her, hated her and yet . . .

Well, he was used to having her around. Anyone would be a little shaken at the thought of never seeing someone they were used to again. Especially someone as lovely as Etta.

He wouldn't think of that. He'd only think of how much he hated her.

He couldn't sleep. He got out of bed, smoked a cigarette, reached for another and found the pack empty. He crumpled it up and flung it across the room. He stood at the window trying not to dwell on how good another cigarette would taste.

It was then that he thought of the gun in his trunk. Old Sid Lester's .32 that he'd used for years in his trick shooting act. It had been mixed in with some other things Dan Ferris had been keeping for him when he died. There'd been no one to turn it over to and the gun had been kicking around in his trunk ever since.

He would tell Jimmy to take it with him when he went to confront Young and Etta. Not that he'd use it but Young was too big and tough for Jimmy to go up against him with no weapon of any sort.

The gun was in good condition wrapped in oiled rags. He'd get it out tomorrow and look it over.

It would make Young look ridiculous, all that brawn reduced to vulnerable flesh told to pack and get out of town. Then, when he was gone, Jimmy could give Etta her marching orders.

Trouble there was, he was apt to be too soft on her, not even call her the names she should be called.

It was too bad his father couldn't take his place. He'd call her plenty. She'd be lucky if he didn't shoot them both, her and her paramour.

135

Jimmy could get away with it but he couldn't. There was no unwritten law to protect fathers-in-law.

What was the matter with him, thinking about shooting? There wasn't going to be anything like that. Jimmy would just carry the gun for his own protection when he confronted them in Grayport.

Jimmy wouldn't even want to take it with him probably, but his father would insist on it, make him face up to the fact that unarmed he was no match for Young.

He'd have a day or two to stiffen Jimmy's spine before Young got settled in Grayport and arranged a meeting with Etta.

Perhaps the best thing to do was to accompany Jimmy and wait in the hall. Prop him up to the last and arrange to stay within earshot so that he could be called as a witness. Jimmy would need one when his divorce case came up.

There was great satisfaction in the thought of branding Etta for what she was in a courtroom. He'd drag her through the mud so that she'd never be able to live it down.

Chapter 14

"Oyez, oyez, oyez!" cried the sheriff banging his gavel. "The Superior Court in and for the County of Grayport is now in session. All rise."

All rose. The judge appeared, severe, bleak looking in his black robes, seated himself and surveyed the crowded courtroom with impassive eye.

The state's attorney for Grayport County rose from his place at the prosecution's table.

The State of Illinois was ready to offer evidence to prove its charge of murder in the second degree against Milton Arthur Young in the death of James Edward Ferris on Friday, July 3 last. The state would show that at approximately 12:15 A.M. on that date the defendant had inflicted a mortal wound on the decedent with a revolver of .32-caliber fired at close range, the bullet penetrating the chest cavity and heart bringing almost instantaneous death to the decedent. . . .

She did not listen to the state's opening address. What had really happened that night almost four months ago was different in many respects from what the state's attorney was saying; in nearly all respects, actually, except the starkest of all: that

137

Jimmy had fallen dead on the floor, blood staining his clothes as he fell.

The state was right about that; it was not right about how it had happened; it was not right about where the guilt of Jimmy's death lay. It did not lie at Milt Young's door even though he and Jimmy had been struggling for possession of the gun when it went off.

The guilt lay at her door. She had betrayed Jimmy for the sake of a passing physical attraction; out of boredom and frustration, contempt for his inability to stand up to his father; out of her own hatred of Dan Ferris, her need to get back at him for the things he had done to his son.

These were the ignoble reasons for her betrayal; these were what had brought death to Jimmy and all of them to the front pages of the newspapers with overworked lurid headlines, actress—she with her stationary part and few lines—and lover, wronged husband, bereaved father, love nests—those dingy little furnished apartments—and the rest. These were what had brought her to this courtroom, star witness for the defense, the newspapers called her, the target of every eye, the prey of every reporter, the scarlet woman of moralistic thunderings.

If there had been better reasons for what she had done would it be quite so hard to bear, the shame and guilt she would carry to her grave?

She had no way of knowing. She only knew that she would have to survive this somehow, do what she could to help Milt and then get as far away from all of it as she could.

The state's witnesses took up the opening day, the medical examiner, the pathologist, the police, the technicians. Defense counsel was frequently on his feet offering objections that were sometimes sustained, sometimes overruled. Splitting hairs, she thought, prolonging the agony, changing nothing.

The second day of the trial Dan Ferris, the state's chief witness, took the stand and for the first time she came to life. She had not seen him since Jimmy's funeral but it was his story, above all else, that had led to Young's indictment for more than manslaughter and now she was to hear it at firsthand.

The state's attorney established his background, his relationship to the decedent and details of the act they presented on the same circuit with the defendant.

"Tell us in your own words, Mr. Ferris, what happened in the last hours of your son's life."

He had long ago got it all in place in his mind, ordered, arranged into a pattern he could live with. He had rehearsed to himself, with all the necessary reversal of roles, what he would say here.

He began without hesitancy, "Jimmy came to me after the matinee and asked me to go and have a cup of coffee with him down the street so we could talk. I'd noticed he'd been a little quiet the past few days, not much to say, not himself—"

Not himself? She leaned forward a little. Why, only the day before he died he'd been so gay and affectionate with her that she could hardly look him in the face.

Dan Ferris continued, "Still, I got the shock of my life when he told me what was on his mind about Etta—his wife, I mean. I couldn't believe at first that she was carrying on with Milt Young. She always seemed the kind that butter wouldn't melt in her mouth and Jimmy worshiped the ground she walked on, never looked at another girl himself . . . "

His pause led the state's attorney to prompt him. "Did he tell you how he'd found out about them, Mr. Ferris?"

"He said he'd followed them to Young's apartment; that they had a system whereby Etta would walk a block or two from the theater to board the trolley and Young would catch it a block farther on. They wouldn't sit together, he said, or let on they knew each other and they'd get off a block apart."

"Did your son tell you how he found out these details, Mr. Ferris?"

"He said he'd get on the same trolley ahead of either of them and sit way back with his hat down over his eyes."

She thought about this while defense counsel objected to the interpolation of hearsay evidence and was overruled by the judge on the grounds that James Ferris was dead and could not give

140

direct testimony himself. She remembered noticing once or twice a man who appeared to be asleep in the rear of the car. It wasn't an unusual sight on a bus or trolley late at night.

Dan Ferris continued, "Jimmy said he would get off at the next stop after them and walk back. He'd see them go into the building, the light go on in Young's apartment . . . "

He wasn't finding this part of his story difficult to tell. Why should he? He hadn't changed anything; he had merely reversed the roles played by Jimmy and himself.

"The light would go out, he said, and Etta would stay an hour or so. Then Young would call a taxi—I suppose there was a phone in the hall—put her in it and send her home."

It was unbearable to think of Jimmy outside watching her betrayal of him. It turned her hot with shame for him as well as herself.

She could not hide her face in her hands with eyes turned on her. She could only look straight in front of her at the wall behind the judge's bench.

"Did your son tell you how many times he followed his wife and the defendant, Mr. Ferris?"

"Three or four times. I'm not sure which."

"But on none of these occasions did he question or accuse her?"

"No. He said it was so hard to believe that he had to be absolutely sure first."

Puzzlement followed shame. How had Jimmy got home ahead of her those nights? She couldn't

141

recall any cruising cabs in the neighborhoods where Milt had rented his apartments and yet Jimmy had always been home and apparently sound asleep in bed when she stole into their room.

How could he have kept it up, his gay, affectionate front with her, while this was going on? She would have been prepared to swear to it that he knew nothing about Milt and her right up until the moment he knocked on the apartment door.

"I asked what he was going to do about it now that he was sure," Dan Ferris continued. "He said Etta had already made an excuse not to go home with him that night after the show so he knew she would be seeing Young. He was going to follow them again but this time, he said, he was going up to the apartment and have it out with them."

"What did you say to that, Mr. Ferris?"

"I urged him — not to." Not was the only word he was inserting into what he had really said.

He closed his eyes for a moment calling to mind Jimmy's paper-white face across the table, his stunned refusal at first to do anything about Young and Etta immediately, his insistence that he had to think it over . . .

It had taken time, anger, derisive goading to bring him to the point of action.

(If he hadn't, God, if he hadn't made Jimmy go, forced the gun into his hand —)

No use to think of that. How could he have foreseen what would happen? It was all her fault.

142

her fault. She had killed Jimmy just as surely as if she'd been the one to fire the gun. If she'd been behaving as a decent wife should, there'd have been no need for Jimmy to seek her out in Young's apartment. Anyone could see that. Anyone would agree with him on it.

Dan Ferris opened his eyes and looked at her, Henrietta Owens Ferris, light woman who had brought his son to his death.

He would never forgive her for it. The law let her sit there, free and clear, and would never call her to account. But he would. As there was a God in Heaven, he would pay her back some day.

The state's attorney paced to and fro in front of the witness stand.

"What did you say, Mr. Ferris, when you couldn't talk him out of confronting his wife and the defendant?"

"I said if his mind was made up to go then he'd need a witness and I was going with him. I said I didn't know what might come of it although"—Dan Ferris's voice faltered, resumed shakily—"I never dreamed that between them they'd kill him like—"

"Objection." Defense counsel was on his feet.

"Sustained." The judge turned an admonishing glance on the witness. "Please confine yourself to facts within your knowledge, Mr. Ferris. Do not try to draw conclusions from them."

"Yes, your honor."

The state's attorney resumed, "What did you

143

and your son do after the show that night, Mr
Ferris?"

"He said he had Young's address and that w
needn't wait outside the theater to follow then
there. So as soon as the show was over we tool
an earlier trolley to Young's apartment and foun
an alley across the street where we could keep a
eye on it."

(Seedy apartment house catering to transient
like the others, catering to sin—not to be re
marked on, though it was Jimmy, not he, who wa
supposed to have seen the others.)

"And did Mrs. Henrietta Ferris and the defend
ant arrive on the next trolley and follow thei
usual procedure of getting off at different stops?

"Objection, your honor," said defense counsel
"The state's attorney is leading the witness an
leading him very deep into the realm of hearsay
Witness is not qualified to testify to the procedur
of earlier meetings or, in fact, offer proof tha
there ever were any."

"Objection sustained," ruled the judge. "Mr. Pa
terson"—this to the state's attorney—"I have a
lowed you considerable leeway in establishing th
background of this case as related to the witnes
by the decedent, but from this point on you wi
please limit your questions to matters on whic
the witness is qualified to give direct evidence."

It took all the self-restraint Dan Ferris coul
manage not to say that there was no one bett
qualified than he to give evidence on the earli

meetings.

The state's attorney reworded his question. "Did
ou see Mrs. Henrietta Ferris and the defendant
rrive at the apartment building?"

"Yes, I did. I saw Young get off the trolley a
top ahead and I saw her get off at the next stop
eyond. I saw them meet outside the building and
o in together arm-in-arm, laughing about some-
ning."

Her husband's eyes, her father-in-law's peering
t them from across the street; she, all unknowing,
aughing, piling fresh hurt on Jimmy . . .

"And then?"

"We crossed the street and went around to the
de of the building. We saw a light go on in back
n the second floor. That must be Young's apart-
nent, Jimmy said. We stood there for a minute
Jimmy having to be urged, prodded to go ahead
rith it when he wanted to reconsider, go back to
ne rooming house, wait for Etta to come home
nd in privacy, just the two of them, confront her
ith her guilt) then went around front and inside.
immy said I was to wait in the downstairs hall,
nat he'd go up alone and call me when he wanted
ne. So he went up and I waited below. I couldn't
ee him after he got to the top of the stairs but I
eard him walking down the hall and went up two
r three steps to hear what when on."

"What did you hear, Mr. Ferris?"

"I heard him knock on the door and say,
oung? This is Jimmy Ferris. Let me in. I know

145

Etta's in there.' Then I heard the door open and close and I went up two or three steps more to where I could see the upstairs hall—"

"Was anyone in sight?"

"No. Jimmy had gone inside. I could hear voices getting louder and louder in there and then what sounded like furniture banging around. I ran the rest of the way upstairs but before I got to the door I heard a shot. I yelled something—Jimmy's name, I guess—as I ran. I threw the door open and the first thing I saw was him on the floor blood staining his shirt—he was dead, just like that—"

He could not go on. There wasn't a sound in the courtroom as he took out his handkerchief wiped away tears and sipped from the glass of water placed in front of him.

Tears stung her eyes remembering that moment but she did not reach for her handkerchief. She did not want to call attention to herself just then when all were looking with sympathy at Dan Ferris. There would be none for her, not her, not anywhere. That was part of her punishment.

The state's attorney waited until the witness regained his composure and said, "Mr. Ferris, where were your daughter-in-law and the defendant when you entered the room?"

"Etta was kneeling on the floor beside Jimmy."

"What was she doing?"

"Nothing. Just looking at him."

"Was she crying?"

"No, just looking. Not a tear."

He did not add that she had been too stunned at that moment to cry or speak or do anything at all. Her face must have shown it but he did not add that. Why should he? He was her enemy. He would paint her in the blackest colors he could.

"And the defendant?"

"He was standing back a little looking down at Jimmy."

"Where was the gun?"

"In his hand."

It had earlier been introduced in evidence, identified as the lethal weapon by the ballistics expert.

The state's attorney took it from the exhibits board and asked the witness if he could identify it.

He would have denied all knowledge of the gun the night Jimmy died, would have said it must belong to Young and possibly have got him indicted for first degree murder if he'd thought he could get away with it. But too many people, including Etta, had seen the gun at one time or another or at least knew about it. He'd had to admit ownership of it from the very first.

The state's attorney led him through the story of how it had come into his possession and then asked, "Did you have any idea, Mr. Ferris, the night you went to the defendant's apartment, that your son had removed the gun from your trunk and was carrying it with him?"

"No indeed."

147

"You didn't ask him if he had it?"

"No, I never gave it a thought."

"You didn't see it in his possession?"

"No."

"In fact, of your own direct knowledge, you'r not in a position to say that he was the one wh took it out of the trunk or that he ever had it i his possession at all?"

"No, I'm not." Dan Ferris looked earnestly the state's attorney and added, "Half the tim whatever theater we were playing, the trunk wasn kept locked, and my son wasn't the only one wh knew the gun was in it. My daughter-in-law kne and maybe Milt Young. There's only their wor for it that it was Jimmy who—"

Defense counsel's loud objections drowned hi out. He was meek under a stern rebuke from th judge. He looked apologetically at the jury. But had made, he hoped, a point.

Etta Ferris did not look at him at all. He ha every right to hate her but not to be as vicious this toward Milt who was, in a sense, the innoce bystander. He knew that any other handson young man with whom she was in daily conta might have taken Milt's place. He knew that t real guilt was hers. It was very wrong for him try to destroy Milt in hitting out at her.

Dan Ferris looked at the jury again, t crushed, broken father who had let his feelings r away with him. The jury was his audience; he f that he was playing well to it.

Defense counsel was cautious and brief in cross-examination. It would not help his client to browbeat this witness in front of the jury.

Dan Ferris stepped down from the stand with a sense of triumph. He'd had some qualms about cross-examination but nothing he hadn't wanted to say had come out in it. Best of all, he had done Etta as much harm as he could. It wouldn't help her now to look sad and beautiful as she sat with downcast eyes waiting her chance to put in a good word for Young and a few more for herself.

Nothing she could say would restore her reputation. The world knew her for what she was, deceiving a decent husband and bringing him to his death.

But desolation followed on his sense of triumph. What good did it do Jimmy to get back at her? He was gone forever. Even if they put Etta and Young behind bars for the rest of their lives it wouldn't bring Jimmy back. Between them they had killed him.

Most of the blame, though, rested on Etta. Young was just her tool, her chance instrument. She was really the one who had robbed Jimmy of his life and himself of his son.

the text across text... was current... might... beside the
different extra... in a sober eye... [illegible] over her. Only
talked of what... with her... the person, not
a man with a... ex... [illegible]... work. She
a... like... though... extra...hope on the over
was nothing... what... talking... [illegible]... over
"Now, [illegible]..."... who... time... the case of Jim...

Chapter 15

She looked briefly at Young as she took the
stand, chief witness for the defense. He did not
quite have the taut, hard-muscled look of the acrobat whose daring feats on stage had first caught
her eye. He had changed, gone a little soft in
these months away from his act. He was very pale,
very grave.

She had not seen him from the night of Jimmy's death until the opening of the trial. They had
talked and laughed together, loved each other in a
light, depthless fashion but now they were two
strangers meeting in a courtroom forever sharing
and forever alienated by the report of a gun and
Jimmy's body falling to the floor between them.

Her paramour, the newspapers called him, her
lover, sweetheart, boy friend, gay Lothario, the
other man. He did not look the part. He looked
like any young man in trouble except that he was
bigger and handsomer than most.

There was no warmth in his eyes as they met
hers. They were two strangers exchanging a passing
glance.

There was no warmth for her from anyone in

the courtroom. Hostility, curiosity or, at best, indifference were in every eye turned upon her. Only defense counsel treated her as a person, not a creature apart.

Her name, occupation, relationship to the decedent were established.

"Now, before we go into the events of July 3 last, Mrs. Ferris, will you tell the court a little about yourself, where you were born, your family background and so forth?"

He had prepared her in his office for the sort of questions he would ask. She sketched it in, born in Greenwood, Ohio, in 1902, an only child, her mother dead since her childhood, her father a druggist, owner of a small drugstore; graduated from Greenwood High School in 1920, kept house for her father and worked part-time for him in the drugstore; life uneventful until the October night in 1921 when Jimmy Ferris, playing at the local theater, came into the drugstore to buy cigarettes. . . .

She was alone at the time, her father having gone home to eat the supper she had left ready for him. She had gone to the show the night before and recognized Jimmy Ferris immediately. He lingered to talk (How overwhelmed she had been by the good-looking young actor, being from another, more exciting world) and she ended up telling him her name and address, a street away from the drugstore.

He was on her doorstep at ten o'clock the next morning and every morning thereafter for the rest of the week. They went for walks between shows in the autumn twilight. The next week he played a nearby town and came back Sunday to spend the day with her. Two weeks later he came back again and this time they eloped.

"How old were you then, Mrs. Ferris?"

"I was nineteen."

"How old was your husband?"

"Twenty-four."

Defense counsel paused to let the jury absorb the picture, small-town girl swept off her feet by attractive, worldly actor, five years her senior and older still, surely, in experience.

(But Jimmy really wasn't like that, ruled by his father, playing small-time Midwestern circuits; now he was dead and it was the small-town girl who had brought him to his death.)

She went on to their married life, the round of rooming houses, the one-week or, in some cases, three-day stands, the new act, incorporating her and Ella, developed by Dan Ferris.

She did not bring out the hostility that lay beneath her outwardly amicable relationship with her father-in-law, the tortuous course of their whole association, complicated further by the contest of wills between them over Jimmy's future.

None of this, except her desire for a more settled life, could be brought out. The rest would

152

vanish like smoke in a puff of air if she tried to put it into words and anything left of it would be of no value to the defense.

But her swift disillusionment with show business, its hardships and uncertainties, came out readily under defense counsel's questions.

"You wanted your husband to give it up, get a steady job somewhere, Mrs. Ferris?"

"Yes. I wanted a home and children." She made herself look at the jury. It might help Milt if some members of it could be persuaded that a scarlet woman had normal aspirations too.

But the jury looked back at her stonily.

"Didn't you enjoy it more, Mrs. Ferris, get a thrill out of being on the stage yourself, after your father-in-law worked out the new act you mentioned?"

"Well, I wasn't much of an actress and didn't have a very big part. The others, particularly my father-in-law, really carried the act."

"But your husband, who'd been in the theater all his life, enjoyed it?"

"Yes."

"And wouldn't give it up?"

"He felt a sense of duty to his father."

"How about your own father? How did he feel about your eloping with an actor and going on the stage yourself?"

"He didn't like it but we became reconciled."

"Has he been helpful to you since your hus-

153

band's death?"

"Yes. He took me away this summer."

(Not to be mentioned was the shock it had been to her father to have her featured in a front-page scandal or the heart attack it had brought on that had kept him in bed the past two months.)

"Is he attending this trial?"

Thin ice but better ventured on in direct than cross-examination with the newspapers mentioning his absence and drawing the inference that it implied condemnation of his daughter.

They did not know about his heart attack or the lakeside hideaway under an assumed name.

"No, he's not well enough to attend."

"You became unhappy, Mrs. Ferris, with your way of life?"

"Yes."

(Bored would be more accurate but more is forgiven stemming from unhappiness than from boredom.)

"And became attracted to Mr. Young?"

"Yes."

Defense counsel took her through their growing interest in each other and made it come out in the guise of true love which it had never been in reality.

At last his questions brought them to the night of Jimmy's death.

No, she'd had no idea that he knew she was unfaithful to him and was following her to her meetings with Young. No, there'd been no change in his behavior toward her. (Other defense witnesses would reaffirm this.) No, she couldn't begin to understand it.

"Then would you say, Mrs. Ferris, that at no time did your husband give you the least inkling of his knowledge that you were being unfaithful to him?"

"Yes, I would say that." She looked at defense counsel in a fresh surge of bewilderment that this was so. She could not add that only the night before his death with the gun already procured, perhaps, and his plans made to confront Milt and her together, Jimmy had made love to her without a sign of jealousy or bitterness.

How could he have done it? She had asked herself this question over and over. It turned him into a different person, someone she couldn't understand at all.

"How did he act the day he died, Mrs. Ferris? Will you tell us, please, about the whole day?"

She had reviewed the day over and over as she had the night that went before it.

"We got up about ten o'clock and had breakfast at a restaurant down the street. There was nothing unusual in my husband's manner. We got to the theater about two o'clock for the afternoon performance which went on after the first showing of the movie. We were billed fourth out of five acts and talked backstage for a few minutes after it was over. Then I went shopping with a theater friend. I'd told my husband she and I would be late and would just have a sandwich or something before the evening show. I didn't see him again until I was getting into costume for it."

"How did he act then?"

She had never been sure, looking back, how Jimmy had acted that night. It was too easy, in retrospect, to read tension and coldness into his behavior. At the time, busy with costume and make-up, she hadn't really paid attention.

Confine her answer to facts. "He didn't say much. I asked him what he'd done while I was out shopping and he said he'd had a sandwich and coffee with his father and gone back to our room."

"Was it unusual for him to do this?"

"No. We often took a nap or rested between performances."

"Then what happened?"

"Someone came into the dressing room—people tended to drift back and forth until it was time to go on—and there was general talk."

"Did you see your husband after the performance?"

"Just for a minute. He said an old friend of his father's was out front and they were meeting him. Then he left." She hesitated. "I noticed, though, that his manner seemed a little strained. He looked at me in an odd sort of way. He seemed

156

keyed up."

"Did you question him about it?"

"There wasn't time. He barely spoke to me and rushed away. To go out front, I thought, to meet his father's friend."

"How was he dressed, Mrs. Ferris?"

"In a dark suit."

"Did you notice any bulge in his clothes or did he have his hand in his pocket in a way that would suggest—"

The state's attorney sprang up to object. "Counsel is asking the witness to draw an inference, your honor."

"Objection sustained."

"I'll reframe the question, your honor. Mrs. Ferris, did your husband have both hands in sight when he spoke to you backstage?"

"No, he had one hand—the right, as I recall it—in the pocket of his suit coat."

This was as close as defense counsel could come to placing the gun in Jimmy Ferris's possession when he left the theater.

"How soon thereafter did you leave yourself?"

"In about twenty minutes or so. I removed my make-up and changed into street clothes first."

"What did you do when you left?"

"I took the trolley to Mr. Young's apartment." She kept her voice as matter-of-fact as she could.

"Was he on the same trolley?"

"Yes."

"Did you and he get off at different stops?"

"Yes."

"Did you and Mr. Young then meet outside the building and go upstairs to his apartment together?"

"Yes." She couldn't keep from lowering her voice.

Dan Ferris's eyes were glued to her flushed face. Little good it did her now to look the perfect lady in her gray suit and tailored white blouse; little good her good grammar and well-rounded enunciation did her; she condemned herself out of her own mouth.

But then she moved her head and a ray of sunlight touched her hair turning it to living gold, making his heart contract with sudden pain, a sense of loss for something that had never been and never would be.

It took him a moment to recover from it and renew his gloating over what she was going through there on the witness stand.

"How long were you in the apartment, Mrs. Ferris, before your husband knocked on the door?"

"Not long. I'd just taken off my hat and was standing in front of a mirror combing my hair when the knock came. Milt—Mr. Young— said 'Who is it?' or 'Who's there?' and my husband said, 'It's me, Jimmy Ferris. Let me in. I know my wife's in there.' "

She paused, steeling herself to relive the next few minutes.

"Mr. Young let him in?" defense counsel prompted her.

"Yes. He looked at me—it was a great shock to both of us—and then unlocked and opened the door. Jimmy rushed into the room closing the door after him. He had the gun in his hand."

"Let's get this all perfectly clear, Mrs. Ferris. Did your husband come to a halt near the door or advance into the room?"

"He advanced a few steps and stopped. He pointed the gun at Milt. He looked—wild. I'd never seen such an expression on his face before."

"Where were you standing at this point, Mrs. Ferris?"

"Across the room. I'd just turned around from the mirror."

"Then what happened?"

"My husband began to threaten Milt. He kept the gun pointed at him. He said it was loaded and that he ought to kill him, both of us, for what we were doing. He said he might . . ." Her voice fell. She swallowed the lump that rose in her throat. After a moment she resumed brokenly, "He wouldn't have though—the gentlest person— wouldn't hurt a fly—I was shocked, yes, but not frightened—"

"You weren't frightened by a loaded gun in the hands of your husband who was wild with rage

159

and jealousy?"

She knew she had said the wrong thing for help
ing Milt but she felt that she owed it to Jimmy
kind, mild Jimmy, to say it.

"No, I wasn't really frightened."

"What about Mr. Young?" Defense counsel wa
guiding her back to the path she had strayed
from.

"He looked very frightened. He didn't know
Jimmy the way I did and thought he meant th
threats he was making. He told him to put th
gun away and then we could talk it all over. Bu
Jimmy kept on pointing it at him. They wer
shouting at each other. I tried to quiet them bu
they wouldn't listen. Then Jimmy took anothe
step, sort of lunged, toward Milt. He jumped him
and tried to get the gun away."

She took a deep breath. "It all happened faste
than I can tell it. One moment they were strug
gling for the gun and the next moment it went of
and Jimmy fell to the floor. His coat had com
undone and his shirt" — again her voice broke —
"turned red. He was dead when I knelt beside
him —"

Defense counsel brought her a glass of wate
and gave her time to collect herself. He took he
through the rest quickly, Dan Ferris's appearanc
on the scene, the people across the hall phonin
the police, their arrival and that of the docto
who pronounced Jimmy Ferris dead, the trip t

the police station, interrogation, Young's detention on an open charge, bail for her, the material witness.

Nightmare relived here on the stand in front rows of listeners.

At the end, pacing up and down before her, defense counsel asked, "Would you say, Mrs. Ferris, that this tragedy, this unfortunate accident came about because you and Mr. Young fell so deeply in love with each other that you could not stay apart?"

There was only one answer to give to that. "Yes." she said firmly.

"That's all, thank you, Mrs. Ferris." Defense counsel stepped back, the state's attorney rose to begin cross-examination.

The judge looked at him and then at the clock. "It's quarter of four, Mr. Patterson. Do you anticipate a lengthy cross-examination?"

"Fairly long, your honor."

"Then we'll hold it over," his honor said reaching for his gavel. "Court will stand adjourned until ten o'clock tomorrow morning."

She thought she had reached the ultimate depths of shame her first day on the witness stand but it was as nothing compared to what she had to face in cross-examination.

The state's attorney began mildly enough taking her back over some of the ground already covered on her background and marriage.

161

He had a heavy, fleshy face. He brought it close to her suddenly and asked, "Did you ever love your husband at all, Mrs. Ferris, or did you just marry him because you were looking for more excitement than you found at home?"

"I married him because I was very much in love with him."

"I see. When did you fall out of love with him?"

"I don't think I ever really did."

"You don't think so? Didn't you testify yesterday that you were deeply in love with the defendant?"

"Yes."

"You stayed in love with your husband and yet you also fell in love with the defendant and broke your marriage vows for him?"

"Part of it was being unhappy because I wanted my husband to leave vaudeville and couldn't get him to do it."

"You regarded that as sufficient reason for taking a lover?"

"No. It — just happened."

"Aside from the fact that your husband wouldn't give up vaudeville, the only means of livelihood he knew, what kind of a man was he, Mrs. Ferris? Was he kind to you? Was he faithful? Considerate?"

Defense counsel rose to object that the state's attorney wasn't giving the witness time to answer questions put to her.

"Objection sustained," said the judge. "Give the witness time, Mr. Patterson."

"He was kind to me," she said. "He was considerate. Faithful. He—"

She stopped short. How could she add that Jimmy was as shallow as a brook barely rippling over its bed, living wholly on the surface of life with no concern for what went on beneath it? Or that she had married his father's obedient son who hadn't the least idea of standing on his own feet?

She couldn't say it. She waited for the next question.

"How many times did you sneak behind your kind, faithful husband's back, Mrs. Ferris, to have relations with the defendant?"

Defense counsel objected that the question was irrelevant, immaterial, designed to embarrass and confuse the witness.

"Your honor," said the state's attorney, "I submit that the question is highly relevant considering that the intimacy between the witness and the defendant led to James Ferris's death."

"Objection overruled," said the judge. "The witness will answer the question."

"We had six or seven meetings," she said keeping her voice steady.

The state's attorney took her through them, the excuses to Jimmy, the precaution of not riding together to Young's apartment, the solitary trips back from it.

It had a dirty sound in her own ears. It was dirty. What madness had possessed her to do it?

Not madness at all; boredom, frustration, emptiness. She must not say that. She must clothe it in what rags of love she could.

It took all morning, the state's attorney merciless in seeking out every detail, objections from defense counsel generally overruled.

After the noon recess the first question was, "Do you still maintain, Mrs. Ferris, that you thought you were getting away with all this and that your husband had no idea of what was going on?"

"Yes, I thought that."

(All roads led to the mystery of how Jimmy could have been so natural in his behavior those last weeks, keeping all that he knew to himself.)

They came to the gun. Yes, she knew her father-in-law had it. Yes, she had seen it at various times. No, she had never taken it out of the trunk herself, never touched it. As far as she knew, Milt Young had never seen it or known of its existence. She had not mentioned it to him. She had not seen or given a thought to it herself for a year or more.

The state's attorney could not shake her on any question dealing with the gun. She had nothing to conceal about it.

She was equally firm on the circumstances connected with Jimmy's death.

At last the state's attorney said, "Mrs. Ferris, I suggest that the circumstances were very different in this regard; that you knew your husband had found out what was going on and that you secured the gun and gave it to the defendant for his protection and yours in the event of a showdown."

"No," she protested strongly. "No, that's not true."

"Oh." He paused. "You mean the gun wasn't just for defensive purposes? As soon as your husband interfered with your liaison the defendant drew it and shot him in cold blood to get him out of the way?"

"No, no," she cried. "It wasn't that way at all!"

Defense counsel stormed objections which were sustained.

Soon thereafter the state's attorney was done with her. It seemed a long way back to her seat.

Chapter 16

The question of who was in possession of the gun was a key point when the case went to the jury.

The state's attorney, in his summing-up, stressed the fact that Etta Ferris and the defendant had as much access to it as the dead man; that there was no disinterested witness to support their story that he was carrying it when he entered Young's apartment. No one had seen him remove it from the trunk and he had made no mention of it to his father. Indeed, his whole life pattern indicated an easy-going disposition without a trace of violence displayed toward anyone. He was not present to speak for himself; it was up to the jury to decide what penalty should be exacted from the defendant who had shot down this kind, faithful husband, cruelly deceived by him and a faithless wife, when he was to confront them with their wrongdoing.

Defense counsel stressed self-defense all the

way.

The judge was more dispassionate in his charge to the jury. He explained the legal definition of murder in its various degrees, the question of malice and intent, laying stress himself on who was armed with the gun at the moment of confrontation. If it was James Ferris, the defendant's right of self-defense against an armed man making threats on his life must be considered; but if the defendant himself was in possession of the gun, then the situation was entirely different. . . .

The foreman of the jury was a forceful man of strong convictions that on this occasion hadn't quite jelled as the case was debated around the table in the jury room.

"It's a funny one," he stated. "If Young had the gun—either took it himself or she got it for him—it would be first degree murder seems to me. He wouldn't need it just to protect himself. From the look of him, he could handle anyone who wasn't armed with one hand tied behind his back."

"He wasn't charged with first," a juror pointed out.

"Of course not. No proof." The foreman frowned at the interruption and continued, "On the other hand, Ferris would know he wouldn't have a chance if they got into a fight and might have figured he needed the gun to even things up."

"There's no proof he had it," said another juror.

"Or that he didn't," the foreman retorted. "That's the trouble: no proof either way."

"The father—"

"Ferris wouldn't tell his father if he took the gun. He'd know he wouldn't let him keep it."

"Mrs. Ferris is a real looker," said a juror. "And built."

Silence of assent around the table. It was an all-male jury. Its members had looked Etta Ferris over on the witness stand. They had solid middle class standards but they had looked her over, putting themselves in Young's place.

The discussion went on but always came back to who had the gun.

There were jurors who believed Young and Etta Ferris's story and jurors who didn't.

On the seventh ballot he was found guilty of manslaughter.

The judge sentenced him to three to ten years in the penitentiary.

Dan Ferris waited outside the courthouse for his daughter-in-law to appear. He did not look at anyone as he went out although many in the dispersing throng looked at him.

He was bitterly disappointed at the lesser verdict of manslaughter, in a rage at judge, jury, lawyers, Young, and Etta. He could do nothing about the processes of the law but he could at least vent his rage on her.

He did not expect her to come out the front door as he had done. She would want to slip out the back way, hide herself, he thought, and made ready for it, moving into the driveway beside the building to keep an eye on the courtyard in the rear.

But she wasn't alone when she came out the back way; she was accompanied by Young's lawyer, got into his car with him and left by a side street.

She could not shed Dan Ferris so easily however. He had trailed her twice to the small hotel where she was staying. He did not know what name she was using there but he would wait for her in the lobby; he would wait till hell froze over if he had to.

He hurried out front, hailed a cab and was driven to her hotel.

The lawyer was just driving away and Etta disappearing into the lobby when he arrived. There was no sign of her when he paid off his cab and strode inside. The clanking of the elevator indicated that she had gone straight up to her room.

He retreated from the lobby before the desk clerk saw him, berating himself for not having got to the hotel ahead of her.

He had to find out what name she was registered under. While he stood outside considering the problem a small jewelry store across the street suggested an answer to it. He went in and bought a pair of cheap earrings, pulled one of them off the cardboard holder and returned to the hotel carrying it in his hand.

"I found this outside," he informed the desk clerk handing it to him. "I think one of your guests, a blonde woman in a gray suit, just lost it."

"Oh yes, Mrs. Parker," said the clerk. "Just a moment and I'll check with her."

The switchboard was in back of the desk. The clerk plugged in room 207, spoke briefly and turned back to Dan Ferris.

"Not hers, she says. She isn't wearing earrings."

"Well, I'll just leave it here. Perhaps one of your other guests will claim it." Dan Ferris removed himself from the lobby to the coffee shop opening off it. He ordered coffee and sat down near the glass door where he had the desk in view.

It was midafternoon. The lobby was empty. Presently, as he had anticipated, the desk clerk vanished into the office that was part of his sanctum.

Dan Ferris immediately got to his feet, crossed the lobby swiftly and took the stairs beside the elevator to the second floor.

In another moment he was knocking on Etta's door.

170

"Who is it?" she asked.

"Message for you, ma'am," he mumbled.

She went pale when she saw who it was and tried to shut the door in his face but he was too quick for her. He got his foot over the threshold and thrust himself into the room closing the door after him.

She backed away turning still paler. "What do you want?" she asked. "How did you find me?"

"No trouble. You're easy to follow, Etta."

"Yes, so I've learned."

She continued her retreat until her hand rested on the telephone beside the bed. "Get out of here, Dan, or I'll call the desk."

"You do that and I'll tell who you are. Then I'll call the newspapers and tell them where the notorious Mrs. Ferris is hiding out."

She took her hand off the telephone. They stood looking at each other, her rapid breathing the only sound in the room.

"What do you want?" she said finally.

"That's better." He advanced farther into the room letting his gaze wander over it. There wasn't much to see. It was a small, nondescript room with one window which overlooked the street, a bureau, bed, easy chair, straight chair, table beside the bed holding the telephone.

Her suitcase stood open on the straight chair. He sat down on the other chair and looked at her steadily, his eyes narrow and cold.

She remained by the bed her hand still hovering over the phone.

"Don't bother," he said. "You're safe enough. I've thought of killing you night and day since Jimmy died and I could do it now, strangle you with my bare hands before help could reach you, but you're not worth the price I'd have to pay for it. You're not worth anything, Etta, you're just a slut, a tramp, not fit for my son to have wiped his feet on—"

His tone was quiet, almost conversational as he went on calling her names, telling her what he thought of her. It was all the more shocking because his tone was so quiet. The names he called her were meant to be shouted, screeched, bellowed in scorn and anger; some she had never heard before.

She sank down on the bed, chalk white, shaking all over, not answering or looking at him. It was just something more to be got through; it was, for him, a release for the anguish and rage and grief he felt. He had the right to pour it all out on her if he wanted to.

He was shaking himself, hands jerking on the arms of the chair. He ran down at last and sat looking at her. In the silence she made herself look back at him.

It held for a few moments and then he broke it.

"Why?" he demanded fiercely, head jutting for

ward. "Why, Etta? You so touch-me-not and then all of a sudden . . . Tell me why . . . for Jimmy's sake. A fine boy like him."

But it was not for Jimmy's sake; it was for his own. Awareness of it lay between them and always had, never to be mentioned, brought out into the light of day.

"I don't know why," she replied wearily. "I'll never know. It—just happened."

"And brought death to Jimmy."

"Yes." As she gave assent it came to her that she had better defend herself a little against this man, violent in accusation, potentially dangerous to her. "But in another way," she added, "didn't Jimmy help to bring it on himself? The moment he took the gun out of the trunk he—"

"No!" He could not let her voice the thought. It was intolerable because, if it came down to who took the gun out of the trunk . . .

"Don't try to put any of the blame on Jimmy," he said harshly. "It all falls on you, you and your paramour, but most of it on you."

He got to his feet and stood over her menacingly. "Young gets three years—he'll be out sooner on parole—and you go scot free. That's how cheap the law holds Jimmy's life. My son, one of the finest young fellows—"

"I know," she sighed. "He deserved much better."

"And you much worse." He came so close to

173

her that she reached for the telephone again and then let go as he walked away, striding up and down the room, beating his fist in the palm of his hand, muttering, half-crying to himself.

Presently he whirled around to her and snarled, "I suppose you'll be visiting Young in prison and waiting for him when he gets out."

She shook her head. "I doubt we'll ever see each other again."

"Oh, so you're running out on him too. Going got too rough for you?"

"It's not that at all. There wasn't enough between us to hold us together and there's nothing left now. He wants nothing to do with me and I want nothing to do with him."

Dan Ferris resumed his pacing, halted in front of her and eyed her wildly. "So you're free as a bird now, you'll get away from all this, find yourself another poor sucker—"

"Will you please go now?" She pressed her hands in exhaustion to her face. She had taken all she could from him. She had to be alone, try to pull herself together, think about tomorrow and all the tomorrows ahead.

"You've had your say, Dan. It's all over now. Nothing can change it."

"No, it's not over!" He glared at her. "It'll never be over until you pay for Jimmy's death. The law won't make you but I will. I don't know how or when or where but I'll find a way if I have to follow you to the ends of the earth to do it."

She looked away from him and did not answer. He marched out of the room slamming the door after him.

She stayed where she was putting her head down on the pillow in the lassitude of despair. There was nothing else to do; there was no hope in the future.

Chapter 17

The ring of the phone brought her to life. By that time the early dusk of October darkened the room. She had to grope for the receiver.

It was her father-in-law.

"Etta?" he said. "This is Dan. I'm afraid I was a little hard on you a while ago. I got upset and let my tongue run away with me."

"It's all right."

"No, it's not. I want to make it up to you a little by taking you out to dinner tonight. Parting friends, so to speak. Letting bygones be bygones."

She was instantly wary. He was too smooth and friendly. Only an hour ago—it wasn't much longer, was it?—he had been glaring at her demoniacally, threatening to follow her to the ends of the earth to pay her back for Jimmy's death.

This change in attitude must fit in with his plan. Now that he'd had time to cool off, he wanted to restore a pretense of friendliness between them. He was afraid he might have frightened her into getting away out of his reach.

His anger hadn't frightened her but this did. She mustn't let him know it though.

"That's very nice of you, Dan," she said. "I appreciate it even though I don't feel up to accepting the invitation. I'm lying down and I'm just going to have them send me up some soup or something from the coffee shop and go to bed."

He protested that she should have more than that; that they could go out right now for an early dinner and she'd be back at the hotel in no time.

"Oh, Dan, I don't feel up to it." She made her tone regretful. "All I want is to get to bed. But if you'll hold your invitation over till morning, we could have breakfast together. Would that suit you?"

It wouldn't suit him but it would have to do. "What time, Etta?"

"Nine o'clock in the coffee shop downstairs."

"Okay, I'll see you then. Good night."

"Good night, Dan."

She sat on the side of the bed after she hung up, no longer listless, marshaling all her energies. She had to get out of here tonight.

She turned on the light and called the bus station. There was a midnight bus to Chicago. She would take it and then backtrack to her father in the lakeside cottage. It had no association with her life and Dan Ferris would never find her there under the name she and her father were using.

She would be safe from him forever once she got away from Grayport.

Where was he now—downstairs in the lobby?

She could be certain he was keeping watch somewhere nearby.

She phoned the coffee shop and asked to have soup, toast and tea sent up. Let him see it being brought up; it would confirm what she had said to him on the phone.

He would still watch and wait but eventually give up and go back to wherever he was staying. He would have to; the coffee shop closed at nine o'clock and he couldn't sit around the lobby too long after that without making himself conspicuous—unless he had moved into the hotel himself.

She called the desk. No, Mr. Ferris wasn't registered.

Her tray arrived. When she had finished eating she drew the shade and packed her suitcase. At nine o'clock she put out the light and raised the shade, settling down to a vigil at the window.

The hotel was outside the business area in a quiet neighborhood. The small shops across the way were already closed or closing. There were few people on the street. Dan Ferris was nowhere in sight but she kept her place by the window. He would appear. He was around somewhere ready to carry out his threat of following her wherever she went.

Did he have the money to do it?

She had no idea. How he had been supporting himself since Jimmy's death or what plans he was making for the future were things outside her knowledge. She didn't know if he still had Ella with him. Perhaps he expected to continue in vaudeville, the two Ferrises, he and Ella.

Would the notoriety build the act up?

She doubted it. In the heyday of vaudeville it might have, but not in its fading days here in the Midwest.

At ten o'clock Dan Ferris came out from under the marquee in front of the hotel, crossed the deserted street and took up his stand in a doorway that commanded a view of her window.

She had raised it a little before she sat down at it. With her room in darkness it would help to make it look as if she had gone to bed. He could not possibly see her but she drew back slightly.

For that matter, she couldn't see him. He had melted into the doorway.

He must have spent the evening in the coffee shop and lobby. By ten o'clock the desk clerk would have begun to cast questioning glances at him. He had then removed himself but he hadn't given up his vigil yet. He had only moved it across the street.

It was unnerving, this invisible watch he kept.

If she hadn't seen him vanish into the doorway she wouldn't have known he was there; he could have followed her, with no suspicion of it on her part, when she left the hotel.

He seemed to be good at what he was doing, almost professional. Where had he got his experience?

The answer came with shattering suddenness: following her. It wasn't Jimmy, never him until the last night of all.

It was Dan Ferris, of course, following her in two or three towns they had played, making doubly, triply sure of her meetings with Milt and then in Grayport telling Jimmy about his wife's affair.

She examined her conclusion and could find no flaw in it. The tormenting question of how Jimmy could have remained so sunny and light-hearted while trailing her to her meetings with Milt was at last answered. He hadn't followed her, had suspected nothing until his father told it all to him at the end.

The gun, too, so unlike Jimmy, was explained. His father had got it out of the trunk and egged him on to take it, preaching self-defense against the hazards of confronting Milt without it.

Dan Ferris, then, shared her guilt over Jimmy. But he would never face it. He never could. He had to put the full blame on her.

It made him all the more dangerous to her.

How long was he going to wait out there? What time was it? She couldn't turn on the light to see.

Without taking her eyes from the doorway across the street she reached for the phone. When the desk answered she said, "This is Mrs. Parker. Will you make out my bill, please?"

"You're checking out tonight, Mrs. Parker?"

"Yes, I'm taking a late bus. What time is it now?"

"It's quarter of eleven."

"Thank you." She hung up and settled back at the window.

Dan Ferris shifted from one foot to the other in his doorway. It offered some protection, not nearly enough, from the increasing chill of the night. He wasn't wearing his topcoat, hadn't needed it during the day, but needed it very much now. He'd catch his death of cold standing around like this. And to what purpose?

None, Etta's darkened window indicated. She hadn't stirred out of the hotel and wasn't going to. She had done just what she had told him: had a tray sent up to her room and gone to bed.

He ought to be in bed himself. He had to get up very early, pack his things and be ready for any move Etta made when he met her for breakfast. He would be there, in case she had thoughts of giving him the slip, not at nine but at seven.

Meanwhile, there was nothing to be gained by

181

keeping this fruitless watch on her room.

He moved out of the doorway, cast a last irresolute glance at her window and turned toward Main Street to catch a trolley to his room.

Etta Ferris watched his departure with relief. When he was out of sight she went into the bathroom, shut the door and turned on the light to look at her watch. It said eleven-ten.

She called the desk again keeping her room in darkness in case her father-in-law was trying to trick her, pretending to leave and coming back.

"Is my bill ready?" she inquired.

"Yes, Mrs. Parker."

"Will you please call a cab for me to be here at eleven-thirty? And send someone up for my suitcase in about fifteen minutes."

"Yes, Mrs. Parker."

She hung up and looked out the window. The street was totally deserted. Even so, she waited until the bellboy was due before she turned on the light to put on her hat and coat and gather up her belongings.

She boarded the Chicago bus twenty minutes later. Promptly at midnight it pulled out of the terminal and soon left the lights of Grayport behind.

She never wanted to see it again. Or Dan Ferris.

He was getting into bed as the bus left. He lay awake for a little while planning the cat-and-mouse game he would play with Etta tomorrow and thereafter until the time was ripe to take revenge on her for Jimmy.

There was no reason for the thought to come to him that almost twenty-seven years would pass before he saw her again.

1965

Chapter 18

Sarah Prince had a talk with the old man the day before she left for her first year at college. She couldn't recall the last time it had happened but it was — oh, ages ago. Hardly ever, in fact, in the past two years since she'd got her driver's license. She saw him, of course, waved as she drove by if he was out on the porch or puttering around in the yard but that was all.

Walking home from downtown that last day she thought about the difference being able to drive made in her attitude. Before she'd had a license it was routine to walk but now, might as well admit it, she felt put upon if she had to.

Amy had walked her four years at high school — didn't seem possible she'd just had her second wedding anniversary — but that was in the old building. The new high school was too far away. Everyone on the street rode the school bus.

What she really needed was a car of her own. Bob had one — he'd paid for it himself, however, working summers for their father—but there was no prospect of her having one in the foreseeable future. Her parents believed it was something you earned the money for yourself and construction jobs like her brother's, paying fabulous rates an hour, weren't open to girls.

She sighed over her carless state but without much conviction. With three cars for four people around all summer she'd usually been able to get hold of one when she needed it. Today was the exception. For one thing, they were reduced to two, Bob having left for college this morning; for another, her parents had gone out separately in their cars, leaving Sarah to walk downtown on her errands.

It was rather pleasant, she discovered, sauntering home in the late afternoon, the September sun warm but not too hot, people in their yards to pass the time of day with, two kittens she wouldn't even have noticed if she'd been driving roughhousing under a clump of shrubbery, a cardinal perched in a tree staring at her impertinently out of his black highwayman's mask and looking away haughtily when she stopped and made faces at him.

So, at last, dawdling on the way, a tallish blonde girl, her hair streaked platinum here and there from the summer sun, fair skin warmly tanned, dark blue eyes showing no trace of the cast for which she had once worn corrective glasses, she came to the house that had been Mrs. Lane's in her early childhood but over the years had become identified with Dan Ferris.

Drawing near, she looked at it as she generally did passing by. She had only flickering memories of Mrs. Lane alive but Mrs. Lane dead at the foot of the cellar stairs she would never forget. It was a scene cut as deep in her memory as an etching cut in metal or glass.

The old man was on the front porch. She called a greeting to him, started to walk past and then, on impulse—was it hail and farewell to a part of her childhood?—went up the walk for a chat with him, noticing on the way how neglected the whole place looked, paint peeling from the siding, missing slats in the shutters, weeds thick in the borders, lawn in need of mowing, the total effect one of decay and encroaching ruin.

The old man on the porch had much the same appearance as his property. His thick white hair that had once been his pride was an unkempt mass as much in need of cutting as his lawn. Beneath it his face had the dried-up look of a mummy's, if a mummy could be pictured with an unshaven stubble on its chin. His eyes had a lackluster stare as she approached. In spite of the mild weather he was dressed in a faded flannel shirt and an old pair of wool slacks. He looked shrunken and frail, his clothes too big for him. His hands, wrinkled skin flabby and loose, rested clawlike on the arms of his chair.

He looked as old as time itself. How old was he? He must be almost ninety, at least not far from it, she thought. But the last time she had seen him close to — when was it anyway? — he had seemed much more alert than this.

"How are you, Mr. Ferris?" she asked climbing the porch steps.

"Fine, fine," he replied his eyes coming waterily into focus on her. "And how are you — uh?"

"Sarah," she said with a smile. "Sarah Prince from down the street."

"Oh yes, of course. Couldn't place you for a minute. Have a seat. How's your folks?"

"Good, thank you." She sat down on the top step. "Beautiful day, isn't it?"

"Yes indeed. Been sitting out here enjoying it."

"I've just been downtown," she said. It sounded pointless but now that she was here she didn't know what to say. For that matter, she didn't know why she had stopped at all.

The old man sat in an old-fashioned rocker with broad arms and a high back. It creaked as he rocked back and forth breaking into the lengthy pause that came in the conversation.

"My brother Bob left for school this morning," Sarah said finally. "It's his senior year."

He obviously had trouble placing her brother but nodded politely and said, "Zatso?" Making further effort he added, "Let's see, you're a pretty

190

big girl now. You must be in high school, aren't you?"

"I was graduated in June, Mr. Ferris. I'm leaving for college myself tomorrow."

"Well, what d'you know," he said. "Time flies. Seems like yesterday I was doing magic tricks for you—" He hesitated. "Was you I'm thinking of, wasn't it?"

"Yes Mr. Ferris. It was a lot of fun." (But it ended with Mrs. Lane dead at the foot of the cellar stairs.)

"Kids always like magic," he said complacently.

She leaned back against the post with a sudden feeling of nostalgia for the child she had been, enchanted by simple tricks, and by this old man she had called the magic grandfather.

But it was all so long ago that from the viewpoint of young adulthood the child Sarah, moving freely in and out of this house, pampered by Mrs. Lane before the old man ever appeared on the scene, seemed another person, a separate self.

She had a snapshot of Mrs. Lane at home. Otherwise, she was a shadow, a figure without a face, except for the day she died.

That day lived full color in memory, the sprawled form, light hair, green skirt and blouse, corner of white clothes washer visible behind her. When she recalled that day, the child Sarah and her grownup self merged into one.

The old man, the third person involved, was

never more than a shadow running down the cel
lar stairs, picking up Mrs. Lane's body, laying i
down again.

Somehow, though, he had lost his magic foreve
that day. She hadn't known why at the time and
still didn't know looking back on it.

Unless it was that in the child Sarah's mind h
was so closely identified with all its horror tha
to avoid thinking about it she had to avoid hin
thereafter.

Years went by before she stopped being afrai
of him. She could not remember ever having bee
inside the house since Mrs. Lane's death. Or, i
she had been, it must have been with her mother
and was so far back that she had forgotten it.

Now the magic grandfather — later, a bogeyma
of sorts — was just a frail old man going senile
living alone in a house as forlorn and neglecte
as himself. There was no magic or fearsomenes
left in him; there wasn't much of anything, in
cluding life itself, left.

He shouldn't be alone like this. He was too ol
for it. It was all very well for the neighbors, he
mother among them, to more or less keep an ey
on him, bring him things to eat, call him on th
phone, but what if something happened to him i
the night, a fall, for instance, alone in the hous
where there'd already been one fatal fall?

But there wasn't anything that could be don
about it. She'd heard it discussed often enough

The old man was adamant about staying where he was, getting upset at the very mention of nursing or retirement homes.

"This is my house," he would shout, "and I'll live in it till I'm carried out feet first."

Lately, it was said, he'd developed the habit of keeping the front door permanently locked. People who went to it were told to go around back and if he let them in at all they didn't get past the kitchen.

Heaven only knew, her mother said, what the rest of the house looked like these days.

She glanced at the front door. In spite of the warm weather it was closed? Did the old man himself come and go by the back door?

The shades were drawn on the living-room windows, she noticed next.

She felt Dan Ferris's gaze on her. "You've grown to be a real pretty girl," he said. "Let's see, you're — uh?"

"Sarah Prince from down the street." (And what was she doing here when he didn't remember her or particularly want her company?)

"And you're leaving for college tomorrow, you said?"

"Yes, Mr. Ferris."

"Never had much schooling myself," he ruminated. "I learned things, though, how to speak right, all kinds of things, from people who knew a lot more than I did. I was quick when I was young. I'd watch and listen and learn."

After a pause he went on, "Did I ever tell you I was on the stage most of my life? Vaudeville. Top billing everywhere I played. All the big-name circuits. Had different acts over the years. Don't rightly remember them all."

He was showing a little more life.

"You were a magician," she reminded him.

He waved it aside. "Assistant to one. Feeling my way in those days. Didn't want to stay assistant to anyone. Then my wife and I—both of us only eighteen when we got married—worked up a song and dance routine and brought Jimmy into it, the dancing Ferrises. Then it was just Jimmy and me until he married Etta. After that I worked up a new act, The Four Ferrises."

"Who was the fourth, Mr. Ferris?"

"Why, it was—" He broke off peering at the girl suspiciously. "If you're trying to get me to tell you about our act you're wasting your time." His voice rose testily. "I won't do it. I won't ever talk about it."

"That's all right," she said soothingly. "You don't have to if you don't want to. Anyway"—she stood up—"I'd better run along now. I've still got loads of packing to do."

"Packing?" His suspicious look deepened. "I can't loan you my trunk if that's what you're after. I keep things in it."

She smiled in reassurance. "I don't need your

trunk, Mr. Ferris. I got a set of matched luggage for graduation."

"Oh. Well, don't let me hold you up." He roused himself to the duties of a host. "Enjoyed your visit. Sorry you won't be meeting Ella."

Ella? Who was she?

Sarah didn't ask.

"Good-by, Mr. Ferris," she said and left, looking back from the edge of the road to wave to him.

He didn't wave back. He sat and rocked and watched her go.

She was glad to get away. She shouldn't have stopped by at all. Nothing could have had less meaning.

She found herself thinking on the way home that Mrs. Lane's first name was Etta. When the old man said Ella was it just a slip of the tongue? Was he so far out that there were moments when he thought Mrs. Lane was still alive?

How sad, how awful, if that were so.

When she got home she looked around her appreciatively. It was good to live in a house where everything was bright and open and right and perfectly normal.

Chapter 19

Sarah and her parents set out early the next morning on the drive to her college, too early for the old man to be out although the girl glanced at his house as they passed it. But then, she was glancing at all the houses on the street, thinking of it with pleasurable melancholy as a form of farewell to childhood and adolescence on her way to the unknown world ahead.

It would be Thanksgiving before she saw this familiar scene again. By that time, she would have settled into college routine, made new friends, absorbed a broader outlook; she would look at her street through different eyes. She was half-sad, half-eager at the prospect; like Janus, she thought, looking forward, looking back.

The old man slipped out of her mind completely. She scarcely thought of him again until she came home for Thanksgiving, Sarah Prince, college freshman, less changed in some ways, more changed in others, than she had anticipated.

She got home Tuesday night and slept until ten o'clock the next morning when the phone began to ring for her. She spent most of the next several hours on it, comparing notes with friends, catching up on local events, making dates and plans for the weekend.

Her brother Bob, wanting to use it himself, demanded exasperatedly of their mother, "Did I carry on like this the first time I came home from college?"

Virginia laughed. "You know girls talk more on the phone than boys."

When he finally separated Sarah from it she drifted out into the kitchen which was filled with the good smells of Thanksgiving dinner preparations and talked steadily to her mother about college, meanwhile picking and nibbling at tomorrow's goodies.

Her mother warned her off a loaf of apple-nut bread cooling on the table. "It's an extra loaf for Mr. Ferris." she said. "I've made him a pumpkin chiffon pie too. I wish you'd whip the cream for it and take them both over to him."

"I hope he's going to have more than nut bread and pie for his Thanksgiving dinner," said Sarah.

"Mrs. Napier is roasting a chicken for him and Mrs. Greene is sending over candied sweet potatoes. He'll be all right. He'll have a good dinner."

"All by himself. Great."

"You know he won't go anywhere. He's been

asked and asked."

"Yes, but that house, the way it's closed up and everything . . ."

Sarah's protest dwindled into silence. There was nothing anyone could do about the old man. It was his house, his way of life.

She felt reluctant to go there. "Let Bob drop the things off," she said but he shook his head firmly.

"I'm leaving right now, got to meet Pickles downtown in five minutes. Besides, the old guy was your pal, not mine."

Resignedly, then, Sarah whipped cream for the pie, put it in a basket with the nut bread, added a bunch of big purple grapes, protested her mother's insistence on her warm coat, submitted to it finally and set out in the gray light of late afternoon on her errand.

The lot between the two houses was still an open field bought by her father to insure his own privacy. He kept the underbrush cut down but that was all. Its tall grass was the drab brown of November and its scattered trees leafless. Through them she could see the old man's house ahead, drawn shades giving it a blank look.

She turned into the driveway heading for the back door out of childhood habit, not because she remembered being told that he refused to answer the front door.

The lawn, now dead, was as unkempt as in

September. Bits of rubbish were caught among the leaves at the side of the house. The amesite driveway had great cracks in it, the garage a broken pane of glass in the door. No car had been kept in it since Mrs. Lane's time.

Sarah sighed in annoyance. Why should she have to get stuck with coming to this depressing place? It was enough to ruin her holiday. Her mother should have made Bob come.

Well, she wouldn't have to stay but a minute. Mr. Ferris wouldn't let her past the kitchen anyway.

She went up on the back porch, rang the bell and realized it wasn't working as soon as she touched the loose button. She knocked on the back door, waited, knocked again.

Wasn't he home? He must be. He hardly ever left the yard.

She knocked again, beginning to worry over his nonappearance. Maybe something had happened to him alone in there.

She turned the knob tentatively. The door opened and she stepped inside.

Immediately she heard voices, the old man's and a woman's. He had company. For once, he had let someone past the kitchen. He was entertaining in the living room.

She hesitated. Should she announce her presence, get involved in identifying herself, introductions if she didn't know the guest, or just leave the basket on the table and have her mother phone him later?

While trying to make up her mind, she looked around her. The kitchen shades weren't drawn all the way. In the fading light that obscured shabbiness and neglect the room touched a chord in her memory. There, under the south window, was the pine table where Mrs. Lane had seated her with things to eat, there were the blue and white cupboards, the double sink, the hanging brass pot that used to have ivy in it, all suddenly remembered, as familiar as if she had seen them yesterday.

She set the basket on the cupboard still of two minds about announcing herself. She was mildly curious about who the visitor was but hadn't been trying to hear the conversation in the living room up until this moment when she must either leave or call out to the old man.

Perhaps she should let him know she was there; perhaps it would look funny, almost sneaky, if she didn't. On the other hand, what would she be interrupting?

For the first time she tried to listen to what was being said or at least hear the visitor's voice which she might recognize.

A few steps took her into the hall. She stopped short as she heard the old man say, "There, Etta, you're all dressed up now. Just let me fasten your necklace . . . My, don't you look beautiful."

Etta, he said. Etta was Mrs. Lane, long dead.

The nap rose on Sarah's flesh. She froze where she stood.

"Thank you, Dan," said the woman's voice. "Show me how I look in the mirror."

"Vanity, vanity," he chided. "Well, just one look."

"I do look nice," said the woman's voice. "Blue's always been one of my favorite colors."

"Matches your eyes." He spoke on a fatuous note. "Sets off your hair. That was the first thing I noticed when Jimmy brought you backstage to meet me. I thought you had the most beautiful hair I'd ever seen. The real McCoy, not like the peroxide blondes a dime a dozen. I always fancied light hair, Etta, although Molly's was dark. Remember how dark it was? No, of course you don't. I keep forgetting she was dead when you and Jimmy were married. You saw pictures of her though."

"Yes. She was very pretty."

Sarah had no memory of Mrs. Lane's voice.

What did it sound like? Who was in there with Mr. Ferris?

She gave herself a mental shake. What a wild thought. Mrs. Lane was dead.

And yet . . .

Nervousness made her breath quicken. She began to take slower, deeper breaths fixing her gaze on the front door. Some light came through the

small glass panes high up in it. On the other sid
of the door was the front porch overlooking th
street, the perfectly ordinary street she had know
all her life. Mrs. Lane wasn't in the living roon
with the old man. She was dead. Sarah had see
her lying dead thirteen years ago.

Who was in there, then, with him? What kin
of a weird game were they playing?

"Jimmy always spoke well of his mother," sai
the woman's voice.

"She was the finest," said the old man. "W
were just a couple of kids when we got marrie
with hardly the price of a license between us bu
we made out all right. Jimmy was born the nex
year, on Molly's nineteenth birthday, as a matte
of fact. I guess you knew that though."

"Yes, he told me."

"We had a good life together, Molly and I
until she was carried off in the flu epidemic. /
good life. It takes a good woman to make a goo
life for a man, Etta."

"I guess it does."

"You guess?" Bitterness sharpened his voic
"That's all you can do. You don't know what
good woman is. Look what you did to Jimmy.

A whimper sounded. "I'm sorry about tha
Dan. I always have been."

"You're sorry, are you? Much good that di
poor Jimmy, shot down by your lover."

Sarah stifled a gasp. What where they talkin

202

about? It couldn't have to do with Mrs. Lane and yet . . .

Who—or what—was in there with the old man?

Ancient superstitions, graveyard tales, turned her ice cold.

She couldn't bear to go look.

She couldn't bear not to.

She edged her way along the wall to the living-room doorway, flattened herself against the doorjamb until she could look with one eye into the room.

The shades were drawn. A dim wall light deepened the shadows, highlighting only the table beneath it. The old man was seated on the sofa facing the door. A beautiful girl with blonde hair, decked out in an elaborate blue cocktail dress, sat beside him.

Sarah drew back after one quick glimpse for fear of being seen. Her heart pounded. There was something familiar about the girl. Something . . .

Memory stirred suddenly. It was Mrs. Lane, restored to youth.

Her head whirled. She pressed her hand against the edge of the doorjamb so hard that it hurt. The hurt was real. It brought her back to reality.

She moved her hand away and leaned against the wall. The girl in the blue dress wasn't Mrs. Lane. Begin with that.

Who was she then?

Mrs. Lane's daughter. Nothing else would account for the resemblance between them.

But how old was Mrs. Lane when she died? Sarah didn't know except that she was older than her mother. It didn't matter. She could have had a late-in-life child.

Her name was Etta too. She had been kept out of sight in her mother's lifetime and since. She couldn't be Mr. Lane's child to be hidden like that. She must be illegitimate.

She had been married. Her lover had shot her husband who was related to Mr. Ferris.

Sarah relaxed as she reasoned it out. She had almost dissolved into panic a few moments ago. It showed what imagination could do to a person. It made her feel foolish.

They were still talking, the old man and the girl, mostly the old man, but Sarah had lost track of their conversation. She shouldn't listen to it anyway. She'd had some excuse for it earlier but not now when she had the situation clear in her mind.

Well, not altogether clear. For instance, why was the girl wearing that fancy dress just to sit there in that dreary dark room with the old man? You'd expect her to at least put the shades up – or were they two of a kind, she as batty as he was?

It was none of Sarah's business. Forget it, slip out the back door and leave the basket outside so that Mr. Ferris wouldn't know she'd been in the house. Her mother could call him as soon as she got home.

But first she'd take another look at the girl.

As cautious as before, she brought one eye around the doorjamb. The old man had turned a little toward the girl holding her hand but she was still sitting in the same position facing the hall, not even glancing in his direction.

Again Sarah drew back quickly for fear of being seen. But her brief look had told her there was something peculiar about her, something that shattered Sarah's newly won calm.

She wouldn't leave just yet. She strained to hear what the old man was saying but his voice had dropped to a mumble and the girl wasn't talking at all.

Something peculiar about her . . . Was it her erect posture, the way she seemed to ignore the old man, not looking at him, letting her hand lie passive in his?

Why should he hold her hand anyway? Was he her grandfather, great-uncle, or how were they related? She called him Dan though. That didn't sound like a relative and not respectful, either, considering his age. Sarah's mother never let her call older people by their first names.

She had shed all qualms about eavesdropping. She had to stay a little longer, try to figure it all out or it would just keep bothering her. It would be like putting a book down without reading the last chapter.

There was more than that involved. There was something peculiar, not just about the girl, but about the whole thing; something so wrong, she realized suddenly, that it was crawly, a little frightening.

She moved closer to the door to listen.

Chapter 20

The old man's mumble continued, occasionally interrupted by a monosyllabic response from the girl.

Sarah, not able to make out what he was saying, jumped when his voice rose suddenly to a shriek. "Did I hear you say yes, Etta?"

"Yes, you did, Dan," said the girl's voice.

There it was again, his first name.

"Let's get this straight: I asked you if you still felt I was partly to blame for Jimmy's death and you said yes?"

"Yes, I did."

The girl had an odd voice, light, lacking depth.

"Just—just because I—I happened to own a gun—" he stuttered in his excitement. "That's it, eh?"

"You know it's much more than that, Dan."

"All right, tell me. I thought we'd had it out years ago but you won't let it rest, will you,

Etta?"

"No, never."

"Go ahead then, say it."

"I'm the most to blame but some of its rests on you."

"You know how it ended the first time you said it, but have your say."

"You followed me when I met Milt. You, not Jimmy. I realized it the night after the trial in the hotel in Grayport—"

"Where you lied to me, gave me the slip," the old man broke in

"Yes, and got clear away too."

"Not in the end, though, Etta, not in the end. I tracked you down."

"You're a good detective, Dan. Jimmy was trusting. You were the one who told him everything."

"My duty, wasn't it? My own son."

Son? Was the girl his daughter-in-law? She couldn't be. It was Mrs. Lane who had married his son.

Two sons, one much younger, perhaps the child of a second marriage?

But the girl had to be Mrs. Lane's daughter with the resemblance between them. Daughter and sister-in-law, too, if she'd married a much younger brother of Mrs. Lane's first husband?

It didn't seem possible. Too tangled. Let it go for now. In her confusion she'd already lost the

208

thread of what went on in the living room.

"No use denying it." The girl's light voice. "All through the trial it puzzled me. Everything was always out in the open with Jimmy."

"That's right. Open, decent, good. Until he lost his head over you. Lost his life."

"But wasn't the father who gave him the gun and egged him on partly to blame?"

In spite of the old man's excitement the girl's voice still held that odd toneless quality. As if reciting, not just saying what came into her mind, Sarah thought; reciting lines spoken many times before.

"No, no," cried the old man. "How many times have I told you not to say that?"

The sofa creaked violently as he spoke. Risking a glance into the room, Sarah saw that he had sprung to his feet and was standing in front of the girl shaking his fist at her.

She couldn't tell if the girl was frightened; he blocked her off from view.

Then he swung around and Sarah had to duck back out of sight.

"None of the blame rests on me," he said pacing back and forth with angry tread. "It's all yours, Ella."

Now he called her Ella—her middle name. Etta Ella was fantastic. Well, Henrietta Ella perhaps.

"There we were, The Four Ferrises, you and Jimmy, Ella and I, a good act built up, everything going along fine until you —"

Etta and Ella weren't the same. Ella was the fourth member of their vaudeville act.

But how long ago? It had to be before the old man came here. Was this Etta a child actress?

"You know what happened the first time you tried to blame me," the old man raved. "You got what was coming to you, didn't you? It took twenty-seven years but you got it."

Twenty-seven years? The girl wasn't even born that long ago.

Sarah's thoughts were in tumult. Actress, face lift, the mysterious Ella rushed in and out of her mind making no sense.

Nothing made sense. She had to get a better look at the girl.

If she knelt down she'd be below their eye level, less noticeable looking into the room.

Her legs, she discovered, were trembling. It was a relief to kneel and take her weight off them.

Her head close to the floor she peered around the doorjamb.

The old man was still pacing up and down in front of the girl hurling accusations and reproaches. With the light fading outside the room seemed even dimmer than a few minutes ago. The girl hadn't moved since Sarah's last glimpse of her. She still sat staring straight ahead with fixed unblinking stare like a robot, like a . . .

Sarah clapped her hand over her mouth to

smother a scream. It was horrible, unbelievable. The girl wasn't real. She was a life-size doll.

The old man had taken up dolls.

She'd never seen one that big before. A mannequin from a department store?

But — a talking mannequin? She shook her head in bewilderment. There wasn't such a thing, was there?

She felt safe looking in at them now, crouched on the floor. The old man had his back turned to her. The eyes she had feared would see her were only glass.

"No gratitude at all," the old man said aggrievedly. "Years of buying you pretty dresses, Etta, and what thanks do I get? You just try to blame me—" He broke off rubbing his hand across his forehead, eying the figure on the sofa and muttering, "I get you mixed up. You're not Etta, are you? You're Ella."

"Am I?" the light toneless voice said.

The old man sank down beside the figure. "Etta, Ella, what's the difference?" He put his arm around it, his hand moving on its back.

The blonde head nodded, the painted lips moved. "How could there be any difference when I was made to look just like her and given almost the same name? We were the greatest, you and I, Etta and Jimmy, me on your lap, Etta on his and the audience laughing, eating up the act. Remember, Dan?"

"Of course." His tone took on melancholy. "I remember every day of it smooth as cream for two-and-a-half years."

Sarah understood at last. It was not a doll, a toy of the old man's dotage on the sofa beside him. He was a ventriloquist and this was his dummy like the ones she used to watch on television. He had cherished and dressed it up since his vaudeville days and now, in his senility, got it mixed up with Mrs. Lane.

It was eerie, spine-tingling but not frightening any more. It would be pathetic if it weren't for the bitterness he felt over his son.

"And then you destroyed it all." He was back on his feet standing over the dummy spitting out his words. "You destroyed the act along with Jimmy. You thought you'd got away with it all when you gave me the slip in Grayport but I showed you, didn't I? The look on your face the day I rang your doorbell was worth the years I'd waited even if I'd just turned around and gone back where I came from."

"But you didn't." The dummy's painted lips did not move although the light voice seemed to come from it.

The old man could throw his voice to it but without his hand working its mechanism to give it a semblance of life it was just a big doll. There was nothing about it to make Sarah feel frightened again and yet she was.

"No, I didn't," he said in triumph. "I stayed to collect the debt you owed me."

"You collected it, Dan. You got twenty-five thousand from me. I couldn't give back Jimmy's life but it was like an insurance company paying, you said."

"That's how I looked at it. Not blackmail. Insurance money."

"But money is all insurance companies pay, Dan. Not a life for a life."

"That was your fault, too, Etta, like Jimmy's death." He stood in front of the dummy pointing his finger at it. "All your fault. The anniversary of the day he died and you didn't even remember it. Twenty-seven years to the day and there you were at breakfast feeling good because I was leaving, thinking about your next date with that fellow you'd met and not a thought, not a regret to spare for my poor son. Was it any wonder— wasn't it enough to—?"

His voice went high and shrill. He grabbed up the dummy, shook it until the dress swirled out around it and flung it back on the sofa.

The blue eyes stared, the painted mouth smiled. Sarah closed her eyes to shut out the sight.

The old man had resumed his agitated pacing when she opened them.

"I had to remind you what day it was," he shouted maniacally. "The anniversary of my son's death and you took a shower and got dressed like

213

any day at all. But you came into my room fast enough when I said I wanted to show you something in my trunk. Remember that, Etta? All the time we were together you wanted to know what was in it. You came across the hall trying to act like it was just souvenirs, scared a little, maybe, but you came. You were a little scared, weren't you?"

"Yes," said the light voice.

"And when you got to the door the trunk was open and there you were—there was Ella, I mean—sitting in a chair all dressed up and I said, 'I want you to meet an old friend of yours—' "

"If I'd some warning—"

"Don't try to excuse yourself! Never try, Etta, because you can't. There was no excuse for the way you carried on, the things you said to me. Say them over now. Say them all."

"I don't want to Dan."

"Say them!"

"All right," the light voice obeyed. "Oh, how could you, I said. Put that thing back in the trunk, Dan Ferris, and get the trunk and yourself out of my house this minute. You're a sick man, sick with guilt over Jimmy, and have been since the day he died."

"That's right, that's what you said," the old man muttered pacing back and forth. "Then what did you say, what other lies came out of your mouth?"

"You said they were lies. I said they were true."

"Never mind that, we've been over it a thousand times already. What else did you say to me?"

"I told you about you following me, not Jimmy; about you giving him the gun and urging a showdown with Milt and me. But why go over it? Like you said, Dan, we've been over it a thousand times already."

"Okay, we'll skip that part. What else did you say, Etta?" His voice dropped to a menacing whisper. "What else?"

"Don't make me say it." A hesitant note came into the light voice. "I'm ashamed, Dan."

"You should be. Say it though."

"No, I'd rather not."

"Say it!" the old man thundered.

The light voice recited, "You're not only sick with guilt over Jimmy's death but over the way you felt about me. I'm no psychiatrist but if you went to one he'd tell you that. I think he'd also tell you that coveting me, your son's wife, Dan Ferris, maybe deep inside you wanted him dead, no longer standing between us."

"That's a lie," screamed the old man stamping back and forth waving his arms wildly. "The blackest lie ever told. Admit it right now."

"Yes, Dan. The blackest lie ever told. But I paid for it."

"As you should. Admit that too."

"Yes, I admit it."

He bent over the dummy. "You admit you got what was coming to you?"

"Yes, Dan."

"That when you started to run out of the room I had every right to do what I did?"

"Yes, Dan, I admit it."

The old man straightened up and gave a long shuddering sigh. He seemed to expel his wildness with it saying reflectively, "I had a right to do it, Etta, but I don't know if I'd do it again. Years here by myself—well, I've had Ella with me, but that's not the same—and I just don't know. For years I dreamed of killing you, I was glad I did it at the time, I felt pretty good getting away with it, but I don't know if I'd do it over again. I don't know if I'd have done it then if you hadn't made me see red with the things you said to me, and if the statue of Thespis hadn't been right at my hand when you turned and ran. I don't know Etta. Funny—the house so empty and all."

"I'm still here, Dan."

"Of course you are." He rubbed his forehead. "I don't know what got into me, Ella. For a minute there I thought you were Etta. But she's dead. She's been dead for years. I killed her."

The old man sat down on the sofa, put his arm around the dummy, drew its head down on his shoulder and began to croon to it gently.

Sarah got to her feet and crept out of the house closing the back door quietly after her.

Chapter 21

She ran down the porch steps but not as a beginning to head-long flight. Although the day was sinking toward dusk there was enough light left to reassure her. The air felt good, chilly, but fresh and clean. She paused at the foot of the steps and drew it into her lungs in deep gulps much as she would gulp water in extreme thirst. It steadied her somewhat but not to the point where she would go back into the house to bring out the basket she had meant to leave outside the door.

She would never go into the house again; she would try not to look at it when she went past. It was a house of evil, a place that should have no reality outside of a nightmare.

But it was real.

She walked away from it down the driveway absorbing and accepting the fact that it was a house where murder had been committed with herself, a small child, involved in it.

Accessory after the fact it was called; innocent accessory in her case but accessory nonetheless.

She was still shaky when she reached the edge of the road. There was a tree nearby and she propped herself against it trying to sort out what had happened thirteen years ago.

One fact was immediately clear: Mrs. Lane was already dead when she herself arrived at the house that long-ago morning to go downtown with the old man. He had killed Mrs. Lane upstairs in his room and then, to build an alibi, had invited Sarah to go shopping with him.

Absently, she bent over, picked up a stick and drew haphazard patterns in the gravel with it while she concentrated on the scene in Mrs. Lane's living room the morning of her death.

It began to come clear in her memory. The shades were drawn just as they were today. Mrs. Lane, dimly seen, lay on the sofa, her face partly hidden by some sort of cloth on her forehead.

She had a headache and they mustn't disturb her, the old man said.

Sarah stood in the doorway with him and made some remark to her, probably something polite about hoping she'd feel better soon.

She was speaking to a dead woman. The answers she received came from the old man, expert at ventriloquism, throwing his voice.

Before that morning, it was a feat he had used so sparingly with her that it hadn't stood out in her mind. His making inanimate objects speak—wasn't there a china animal he had mostly practiced it on?—was just one accomplishment among the many with which he, the magic grandfather, had awed her small self.

If she had mentioned it at home her family, bored to tears, no doubt, with hearing about the wonders he performed, probably hadn't listened to her.

No one, it seemed, had known at the time. Certainly not from Mrs. Lane, considering that it was connected with the scandal she was paying blackmail to cover up. The old man would keep quiet about it too. It must have been in the newspapers at the time it happened and he wouldn't want to take the chance that his ventriloquism would ring a bell in someone's memory. That would be killing the goose that laid the golden egg.

Sarah drew squares in the gravel, rubbed them out with her foot and drew circles. Her hands felt cold. She dropped the stick and shoved them into her pockets but made no move toward going home.

She was still turned inward, lingering morbidly over the image she conjured up of the child Sarah talking to a dead woman—but surely not paying much attention in her eagerness to set out for downtown?—with the old man a watchful figure beside her, speaking for Mrs. Lane who would never speak for herself again.

What would he have done if she'd run over to the sofa and found out the truth?

He wouldn't have let her. He probably had her by the hand.

Were Mrs. Lane's eyes open?

She shivered. As she remembered it, it seemed that they were.

But she couldn't remember much of the rest, she realized, as she forced her thoughts past that macabre detail; just that after they'd said good-by to the cold flesh—or was it still warm?—on the sofa, the old man had got her out of the house ahead of him.

It wouldn't have taken him long to throw or drag Mrs. Lane's body down the cellar stairs.

She had a vague memory of the policeman who asked her how long she had waited outside alone. She had been told that she was questioned by him but remembered virtually nothing else about it.

Or about the shopping trip downtown. She knew most of it from hearsay, the toy dog the old man had bought her, their lunch at the inn, but the one thing she remembered about it herself was his buying the pocketbook for Mrs. Lane. Somehow that remained, the old man taking his time as he made his choice, knowing full well he would return it to the store, looking sad and bereft while the saleswoman expressed sympathy.

221

Eventually they were back at the house and he had let her, a small child, discover the open cellar door . . .

She had been the ideal tool for his purpose and the old man, the terrible old man, had not hesitated to use her every step of the way.

He had got away with blackmail and murder and stayed on in his victim's house to become an object of solicitude among the neighbors, poor old Mr. Ferris, all alone in the world.

They didn't know, of course, about Ella.

Sarah detached herself from the tree and turned toward home, its lights shining out across the field in day-and-night contrast to the darkened, ghost-ridden house she had left behind.

But she did not hurry toward the beckoning lights. She moved at a snail's pace, head hunched forward, shoulders slumped in a posture her mother was quick to reprimand, pondering what she had learned.

What could be done about it, an old man, one foot in the grave, babbling to a dummy about a murder he'd committed thirteen years ago?

She'd heard him admit it, give details, but if the police were brought in to it, the first thing they'd ask was how reliable he was; he's crazy as a loon, they'd say.

It would just make a big fuss that would come to nothing.

On the other hand, murder was murder. There

was the moral issue, thou shalt not kill, involved.

But the old man had killed and all these years got away with it. Well, got away with it as far as the law was concerned; but not from what she'd seen, to live happily ever after.

She sighed. Half a term of introductory psych wasn't much of a background to bring to bear on his behavior, but it seemed as if almost anyone ought to be able to figure out some of it: at the very least, that the dialogue the old man carried on with himself through the medium of Ella wasn't something new in his life.

Behind drawn shades and locked doors it had been going on for years.

Ella was his conscience; she was Mrs. Lane; she was a link with his son. She was the symbol of some love-hate thing far beyond Sarah's understanding. She was conqueror and victim; the old man's albatross and his unattainable goal. She was some final shape of horros from which he couldn't — or perhaps didn't want to — escape.

What did he say in the stores when he bought Ella a new dress? For my daughter, my granddaughter, my niece — or for my idol, my fetish, my avenging fury?

Sarah shivered. She had to stop it. Ella would haunt her enough without embellishments of her own.

The lights of home were just ahead.

What should be done about the old man?

Her mother opened the front door to take in the evening paper and waited in the doorway as she saw Sarah approach.

"Well, you were gone long enough," she said. "You must have had quite a chat with Mr. Ferris."

Sarah looked at her mother's firm-lipped, intelligent face. Here, of course, was the answer. Of course. She hadn't lived long enough, didn't know enough to make a decision on this. She would shift the burden to her mother and her down-to-earth father, let them decide what should be done about it.

"Oh, Mother," she said and clung to her as they went into the house.